Puffin Books

Editor: Kaye Webb

KU-739-839

15

THE WOMBLES AT WORK

'Tobermory,' said Great Uncle Bulgaria Womble
seriously, 'I'm worried.' It didn't seem much to worry
about, just that young Orinoco had trodden in a patch
of diesel oil and was suffering now from falling fur,
but Bulgaria could see it happening to all his tribe
unless something could be done to stop the humans
in their crazy race to pollute the world with dirt and
poisonous chemicals.

'Hold on,' said Tobermory, just longing to get back to
his Workshop, 'If Human Beings are so silly that they want
to poison themselves, well that's their affair!'

Later on, however, Tobermory had to admit that
Womble Conservation Year with a Gold Medal for
the best anti-pollution idea wasn't such a bad scheme
after all, for it did help the busy Wombles to clear up
the rubbish in Hyde Park better than ever before, and
led to some really useful and extraordinary
discoveries ...

Everyone knows the Wombles, but maybe you don't
know that there are two other books about them in
Puffins: *The Wombles* and *The Wandering Wombles*.
There is also a Young Puffin, *The Invisible Womble
and Other Stories*, and two Picture Puffins, *The
Wombles in Danger* and *The Wombles Make a Clean
Sweep*. Another Puffin by Elisabeth Beresford is *The
Secret Railway*.

Elisabeth Beresford

The Wombles at Work

Illustrated by Barry Leith

PUFFIN BOOKS

Puffin Books, Penguin Books Ltd,
Harmondsworth, Middlesex, England
Penguin Books Australia Ltd,
Ringwood, Victoria, Australia
Penguin Books Canada Ltd,
41 Steelcase Road West, Markham, Ontario, Canada
Penguin Books (N.Z.) Ltd,
182–190 Wairau Road, Auckland 10, New Zealand

First published by Ernest Benn 1973
Published in Puffin Books 1975

Made and printed in Great Britain by
Cox & Wyman Ltd, London, Reading and Fakenham
Set in Linotype Pilgrim

Contents

To Max with Love

1   Great Uncle Bulgaria's great idea

Dawn was just breaking over Hyde Park – and the rest of London of course – when Tomsk Womble slid back the bolt that fastened the front door of the Wombles' underground burrow. It's a very large burrow, as it has to be because a great many Wombles live there. The Womble in charge of this particular burrow is Great Uncle Bulgaria. He's so old that his fur has turned snow-white and he has to use two pairs of spectacles; and also because of his great age he feels the cold a bit, so he wears a tartan shawl to keep out any possible draughts. He's rather strict and if any young Womble misbehaves Great Uncle Bulgaria has a way of looking through both pairs of spectacles which always makes that particular young Womble shiver in his – or her – fur.

Apart from Great Uncle Bulgaria's study, in the burrow there are bedrooms and dormitories, a play-room, a dining-room, a good big kitchen where Madame Cholet Womble produces some delicious meals, a Womblegarten – which is run by Miss Adelaide Womble who stands no nonsense from anyone – and a whole series of store-rooms and a Workshop which are presided over by Tobermory.

The Wombles say that Tobermory can either mend or make use of any piece of rubbish that they pick up and bring him. It was his expert grey paws which mended the broken rockers on Great Uncle Bulgaria's rocking-chair by covering them with sliced-in-half rubber tyres and it was Tobermory who invented a way of growing toadstools – of which the

Wombles are particularly fond – on damped down news-papers and bus tickets. With the help of Miss Adelaide, he had even organized a special tidy-bag for every working Womble, for like all the Wombles he can't abide waste and the way in which Human Beings throw away, and leave lying about, so much litter constantly amazes him.

But then it astonishes all the Wombles, for they are the tidiest and the most careful creatures in the world and one of their favourite sayings is, 'What a human being throws away in a *day* a Womble can live on for a *month*!' While Great Uncle Bulgaria, over a sip of nettle juice syrup, has often said:

'If it wasn't for us Wombles clearing up all the mess that the Human Beings leave behind them, the world would be covered in rubbish, rats, flies and pollution and all kinds of illnesses by now. It's an absolute disgrace the way they dump their litter!'

All of which was very far from the mind of Tomsk Womble as he came out of the burrow and sniffed the early morning air. He had a neatly mended towel slung round his furry shoulders and he was whistling softly to himself, his little black eyes shining with happiness.

'It's going to be a lovely day,' Tomsk said to himself, 'a love-erly day for a swim-te-tim-te-tim . . .'

He put his sharp nose round the door and sniffed the cold morning air which, even in London, has a fresh unused smell about it at this early hour. Then he wriggled his way through the bushes which hid the front of the burrow from the prying eyes of any inquisitive Human Beings and took a quick look round to make sure that there was nobody about.

There was a thin white mist lying just above the grass so that it looked as if the Park was covered with a nice comfortable shawl. Two grey ears appeared over the top of this shawl and then a round, munching face with round black eyes and white whiskers.

'You're not nobody,' said Tomsk. Words which would have made Great Uncle Bulgaria groan, but the rabbit seemed to understand their meaning for it stopped eating and then with a flick of its back paws it was gone.

'Silly things, rabbits,' said Tomsk, 'got no sense at *all*. Can't even *swim*. Te-tum-te-tum-te-tum. One, two, one, two and away ...'

Tomsk was the largest of the Wombles and also by far and away the most energetic. He was very good at all games and when the Wombles had first moved to Hyde Park he had missed his morning round of golf a great deal.* Like many of the Wombles, he had been tempted to return to Wimbledon Common. But now they were all settled into their new burrow, there was no more talk of moving back. Tomsk had discovered the Serpentine, a stretch of water much larger than Queen's Mere in Wimbledon and he had decided to take up long distance swimming instead. All Wombles are natural swimmers, but Tomsk, with the aid of a little booklet called SWIMMING AND DIVING (*Advanced Course*), was learning to do all kinds of fancy strokes.

He folded up his towel and put it neatly on a seat and then put one paw into the water.

'Lovely,' said Tomsk, although it was extremely cold. 'Morning all.'

The two swans, a tufted duck and a group of mallards, to whom this remark was addressed, either waddled or paddled away; and, if he hadn't been so busy about his own affairs, Tomsk just might have noticed that for the second week running one of the swans was looking far from well. Tomsk strode into the water until it reached as far as his round stomach and then put his front paws together and did a neat little duck-dive which made hardly a ripple He swam under

* See *The Wombles, The Wandering Wombles*.

water for a while, but it was rather cloudy and so he came up to the surface, took a deep breath and, carefully reminding himself of Chapter Three in the booklet, started on the butterfly stroke.

Tomsk went through the water looking for all the world like some round, furry little power-boat and a heron which had just settled itself in its comfortable winter quarters on the Serpentine Island, rose out of the bushes with a great flapping of its large wings.

'Silly things, herons ...' puffed Tomsk, rolling on to his back and gasping a bit, before starting on another stroke.

The heron flapped up higher, wheeled round and then, to Tomsk's surprise, came whizzing down towards him with its long neck stretched full out.

'Whoops,' said Tomsk and made for the safety of the bottom of the lake. It was extremely muddy, but Tomsk was in too much of a hurry to bother about that or to notice the fish, which for some weeks now had not been quite their usual quick-moving selves.

But he had set himself a full half-hour's swimming exercises and the heron soon got tired of the job of pretending to swoop on him; so the sun was starting to glint palely over the tops of the trees by the time Tomsk climbed out of the water. He towelled himself briskly – exactly in the way shown in the booklet although Wombles being furry just dry

out naturally anyway – and then doubled back towards the
burrow, with his elbows into his sides and his chin held
up.

'Lov-erly swim te-tim-te-tim-te-tim . . .'

'Oh do shut up. Do!' said a cross voice.

'Te-tum-te-what?'

'Shut up. Up shut.'

Orinoco, the fattest, the laziest and quite the greediest of
the Wombles, was standing in the doorway of the burrow
with his dreadful old hat pulled down over his sleepy eyes,
and his scarf wound round and round his fat neck. Grasped
in one paw was his Womble tidy-bag, for Orinoco was on
early clearing up duty this particular week. He was not very
keen on work at the best of times and the early morning
shift was his most unfavourite. First of all because it meant
he had to roll out of his nice cosy bed so early in the day;
and secondly because he knew very well that, Human
Beings being the untidy and wasteful creatures they are,
there'd be a great deal *to* clear up.

'And thirdly,' Orinoco muttered to himself, 'Tomsk
always looks so fit!'

He didn't feel at all well himself and his back paws were
starting to itch again. *And* his shoulders. And his elbows and
really, now he came to think of it, all of himself.

' 'Course I'm fit,' said Tomsk, running up and down on the
spot. 'If you weren't so fat, you'd be fit.'

'Ha!'

Orinoco went slowly on his way and then paused by a
nice thick bush and rubbed himself against it, as he said over
his shoulder:

'Here, hoi, you, Tomsk. Did you see a copy of *The Times*
anywhere? Great Uncle Bulgaria wants it.'

'No, sorry Orinoco. Now if you came swimming with me
every morning you'd feel . . .'

'Grrrr,' said Orinoco and stopped rubbing himself and

plodded off to start work. It was just as he had feared: the piece of the Park for which he was responsible was littered with all kinds of rubbish. Tins and packets, paper-bags and milk cartons, bus tickets and iced-lolly sticks, sweet papers and newspapers. Orinoco rammed them all into his tidy-bag, stopping now and again to have a good scratch, and then his luck turned and he found a rather crumpled copy of *The Times* newspaper lying on a bench. He smoothed it out, folded it and gave himself a couple of rubs against the back of the bench and then, for him, trotted quite briskly back to the burrow where Tomsk was now on duty as the Day Watch Womble.

'You're back quickly,' said Tomsk. He had his tongue caught between his teeth because he had to think hard when he was marking Wombles in and out on duty. He swam very fast, but he did read rather slowly. And he wrote even more slowly.

'Here ...' Tomsk went on, 'you've only been working – um – two and four make – um – well about twenty minutes. You can't be back yet.'

'Well I *am* back *and* I've got a copy of *The Times*. That's priority you know.'

'Pri-what?'

But Orinoco was already bustling down the passage in a very important manner, so Tomsk stuck his tongue out of the corner of his mouth in order to think better, crossed Orinoco's name off in the Duty Book and then very carefully wrote down the time.

'Come in,' said the gruff voice of Great Uncle Bulgaria as there was a gentle tap on his sturdy door. 'Oh it's you, young Womble, and what do you want?'

'I've been very busy Great Uncle Bulgaria,' said Orinoco, 'and *while* I was very busy I found a copy of *The Times* lying on a bench.'

'*The Times*,' said Great Uncle Bulgaria sternly, as he

looked over the spectacles on his nose, '*Never* lies. You can depend upon it for the truth, however bad that truth may be. Thank you, Orinoco, and do, for goodness sake, stop scratching yourself. When did you last have a swim?'

'It was . . . it was just the other day.'

'Ho hum, I see. All right, although it's early I can see you've picked up quite a lot of rubbish – tck tck tck, Human Beings are the untidiest creatures in the whole world – so you can go and have your breakfast.'

Orinoco mumbled a 'thank you' and turned away.

Great Uncle Bulgaria, who was shaking out the pages of his newspaper, glanced over his shoulder and said sharply:

'Breakfast – Orinoco. *Food.*'

'Ummm,' said Orinoco.

'It's toadstool pie with elm-leaf sauce.'

'Ummmmm.'

'Don't you feel well?' asked Great Uncle Bulgaria, his voice growing sharper than before.

'Not exactly. But not exactly ill either. Just you know.'

'No I *don't*! Not unless you tell me. Please explain properly Orinoco!'

'Well I'm sort of itchy.' Orinoco said miserably, 'and some of my fur's coming out and my back paws hurt a bit. It's not that I'm *complaining* . . .'

'Ho hum. Let me see those back paws.'

Orinoco hung on to Great Uncle Bulgaria's desk and lifted first one paw and then the other, while the old Womble inspected them through both pairs of spectacles, going 'Hm, hm, hm' under his breath in such a serious way that Orinoco became quite alarmed.

'I'm not really ill, am I?' he asked in a squeaky voice, 'not really properly ill? Because . . .'

'No, of course not, you silly young Womble, but you've been walking on diesel oil and it's got into your skin. It can be poisonous if . . .'

Orinoco went pale under his fur and shivered.

'Stop wriggling,' snapped Great Uncle Bulgaria, giving poor Orinoco a gentle tap with his stick. 'It can be poisonous if it's absorbed in very large amounts. You've only got a very little bit stuck to you. Is anything else wrong with you?'

'Yes,' said Orinoco sadly. 'I'm not hungry all the time. Not like I used to be.'

'Dear, dear, dear me! I never thought the day would come when I'd hear you of all Wombles say that! Well I don't suppose it's overwork, not in your case. The diesel oil must be making you feel out of sorts. Orinoco, go and see Madame Cholet and ask her for some of her special fur ointment and a double dose of daisy-and-dandelion and on your way please call in on Tobermory and say that I should like to see him.'

'Yes, Great Uncle Bulgaria.'

Orinoco gave himself a final gentle rub against the door-post and then vanished, leaving Great Uncle Bulgaria to stare at the door with a worried crease between his white eyebrows.

'Probably do him good, not to eat so much for a bit,' he muttered and turned back to his newspaper. The crease, however, instead of vanishing as Orinoco had done, grew more and more furrowed until by the time Tobermory arrived it was very deep indeed.

'Morning,' said Tobermory, coming into the room and pushing his screwdriver behind his ear so that he could hold his paw out to the fire. 'Winter's coming and I've got a lot to do, so what is it now?'

'It's not a *good* morning,' said Great Uncle Bulgaria. 'Sit down old friend.'

'All right, but only for a minute. Young Orinoco looks out of sorts . . .'

'Falling fur and loss of appetite.'

'Tck, tck, tck, that's bad.'

'It is. Tobermory, I'm worried.'

'Never knew you when you weren't. What is it now? As I said . . .'

'You're busy. I know. But stop thinking about your Workshop and listen to this for a minute.'

Great Uncle Bulgaria held *The Times* at paw's length and shook his head slightly so that both pairs of spectacles settled firmly on his white nose. He read out loud:

' "With Concern for Tomorrow . . ." '

'That's Tuesday. What so special about Tuesday . . .?'

'It's the headline of this article. Just listen. "We are facing Doomsday. In this over-populated world we face a new enemy, an enemy which the world has never known before – pollution. Pollution of the sea, in the atmosphere and on land. Never before has the controlling of rubbish and effluents . . ." '

'Effluents?'

'Drains and waste things . . .'

'Ah . . .'

' "Or the safe transport, formulation and use of oil and chemical products" . . .'

'Eh?'

'*Not* dumping tins and barrels of harmful chemicals.'

'Ah.'

' "And last but by no means least banning the piling up of rubbish which . . ." '

'That's us,' said Tobermory. 'All right, Bulgaria. I quite see that all this pollution business is going on all over the world. But Womble-wise there's precious little we Wombles can do about keeping the sea clean or stopping noisy aeroplanes or the dumping of harmful chemicals and stuff like that! Our business is to clear away the rubbish that Human Beings leave behind 'em. And I must admit a more wasteful lot of creatures I've never met. But . . .'

'But, old friend, we Wombles must do what we can. I agree with you entirely that Human Beings are quite ridiculous. They seem to be determined to choke themselves to death, but it's up to us Wombles – as it always has been – to

try and stop them. Doomsday is coming, Tobermory, unless WE do something.'

'Hold on,' said Tobermory, who was used to Great Uncle Bulgaria working himself up into a state. 'We Wombles do more than our bit to stop pollution and all that rubbish, if you'll pardon the phrase. *We* don't live in their cities or towns. Our lives are down here in our burrows. And a very nice burrow this is, too, since I got the lighting and heating going properly – even though I say it myself. If Human Beings are so silly that they want to poison themselves, well that's their affair, not ours!'

'Old friend, old friend,' Great Uncle Bulgaria said sadly, 'these silly Human Beings will take us with them. Already Orinoco has falling fur, all kinds of itches and a nasty case of diesel paw, not to mention loss of appetite. Now Tobermory, you must admit that if Orinoco can't eat until he almost bursts there *must* be something wrong?'

'Orinoco? You mean he's caught this illness from pollution?'

'Exactly. It must be poisoning from the diesel oil. Of all of us Wombles he would be the last to stop feeling hungry.'

'Oh dear.'

'Ho hum. So we must do *more* than out bit. We are all in deadly peril and to save ourselves and all other living creatures we must fight this enemy on the beaches, in the fields...I have made up my· mind Tobermory. We Wombles must redouble our efforts to make Britain – indeed the whole world – clean and beautiful again.'

Great Uncle Bulgaria heaved himself out of his rocking-chair and pushed one paw into his tartan shawl and his voice took on a deep, dramatic growl as he went on:

'Yes, we shall fight the enemy on the beaches, in the streets and wherever they happen to be. We shall brook no defeat ...'

'Oh dear, oh lor,' said Tobermory, scratching behind his

ear with his screwdriver, 'Oh dear, oh dear and just when I was ...'

'In fact I shall make a little speech tonight,' said Great Uncle Bulgaria resuming his natural voice. 'About the duties of us Wombles and – and – well never mind that now. All right Tobermory?'

'I suppose so.' Tobermory shook his grey head and shuffled towards the door and then scratched behind his other ear. He knew all about Great Uncle Bulgaria getting one of his great ideas.

'Oh dear, oh dear, oh dear,' sighed Tobermory. 'Here we go again ...'

Tomsk and the sick swan

Great Uncle Bulgaria's latest great idea passed happily over the heads of most of the Wombles who were gathered together to hear him that evening.

'It's only about doing more work,' said Bungo softly. 'And I think we jolly well work hard enough already, don't you Tomsk?' Bungo was easily the most bossy of all the young Wombles in the burrow.

'Mmmm.'

Tomsk was very sleepy after his long day and his head fell heavily onto Bungo's shoulder and his mouth gaped open in a snore which luckily Bungo was able to stop with his front paw, so that only a kind of snort emerged.

'And so I have decided,' said Great Uncle Bulgaria, looking over his spectacles in the direction of this strange muffled sound 'to present a medal, a *special* medal, a *gold* medal, to any Womble who produces the best anti-rubbish, anti-pollution result or idea in this Womble Conservation Year.

'Like the Olympic Games?' said Tomsk, suddenly coming awake.

'Well – er – yes. Just like the Olympic Games,' agreed Great Uncle Bulgaria, a bit cross that he hadn't thought of this before himself. 'I now declare this meeting over,' and he clapped his paws and began to hobble off the platform, leaning heavily on his stick.

'One moment please, Great Uncle Bulgaria,' Miss Adelaide Womble who was in charge of the Womblegarten, got to

her back paws. 'I have a question. Are *all* Wombles, no matter what their ages, free to take part in this contest?'

Great Uncle Bulgaria, who hadn't thought of this point either, hesitated and then shuffled back to the centre of the stage.

'Certainly, Miss Adelaide,' he said firmly.

'Ah HA,' said Miss Adelaide and sat down.

'That's not fair,' said Bungo under his breath. 'They're only little Wombles. They haven't even got names yet . . .'

Which was perfectly correct as it isn't until the Wombles are judged to be old enough and sensible enough to go out of the burrow and to start clearing-up work, that they are also allowed to choose a name for themselves from Great Uncle Bulgaria's old atlas.

'It's perfectly fair,' said Miss Adelaide, who had overheard this remark. She turned and looked at Bungo in a way which made his fur stand on end all over his tubby little body; and he suddenly stopped feeling like a working Womble of the world and felt instead exactly as if he was back in the Womblegarten and having trouble with decimalization sums.

'But . . .' said Bungo in a very small voice.

'That's enough of that,' said Miss Adelaide. 'You, Bungo, may think – although I doubt very much if you ever do any such thing – that rubbish is only dumped *on* the ground. Well let me tell you that a great deal is shovelled underneath the ground, which is where my young Wombles can do their work. Bungo indeed! I always said it was a silly name, but it suits you to a W.'

And Miss Adelaide swept out of the hall with all the little Wombles laughing and shuffling their paws as they followed her.

'I don't care,' said Bungo, who did. 'I'm not interested in any silly old competition. I'm going to see poor old Orinoco ...'

Orinoco was sitting up in bed and feeling very sorry for himself. He looked terrible. He was covered in ointment so that his fur was all greasy and, for him, he was almost thin although by normal Womble standards he would be considered quite well covered.

'I've got falling fur and diesel paw,' he said huskily.

'What's that?'

'I don't know, but I've got it and it's very nasty. It takes your appetite away for a start. Madame Cholet brought me scrambled dandelion pie for my supper tonight and I didn't even fancy it. I only had a couple of mouthfuls ... well, perhaps six mouthfuls and I had to *force* them down.'

'I say Orinoco,' said Bungo, rather alarmed, 'I tell you what, I'll go and get you your favourite book out of the library, Fortune and Bason's *Splendid Christmas Catalogue* for 1932. The one with all the chocolate truffles in it. *That*'ll cheer you up, old Womble.'

'No it won't. I'm off food altogether, you know ...'

'You can't be. Not you of all Wombles.'

'I can be, if I want to be. Leave me alone ...'

Bungo, now very alarmed indeed, tip-toed towards the door and then stopped as a faint voice from the bed said weakly:

'However, dear friend, if you *insist*, I might just fancy a small, a *very* small sip of buttercup broth. But not if it's too much trouble . . .'

'No trouble at all,' muttered Bungo and dashed off to the burrow kitchen to find Madame Cholet, that excellent cook, who was cleaning the stove so that it would be ready for tomorrow morning's breakfast.

'Buttercup broth,' murmured Madame Cholet. 'Yes, I can manage that, I think. Poor little Orinoco needs to keep up his strength, eh?'

'Well, he's not *exactly* little. He's quite fat really.'

'He will become very little if he stops eating.'

Madame Cholet hurried off into her pantry and came back with a tin which had once held a fizzy drink, but had since been scoured out and re-christened, 'Buttercup Broth'.

'You mean he could get smaller and smaller?' Bungo asked with interest.

'Thinner and thinner,' corrected Madame Cholet and added, 'drat, all the heat's gone out of the stove. Poor little Orinoco will have to make do with a buttercup shake instead.'

'Can I warm it up for you?' asked Bungo, not entirely out of the kindness of his heart, as he had learned some time ago that if a Womble helped Madame Cholet in the kitchen, he or she was often rewarded with a nice tasty tit-bit of this or that.

'No you can't. It's not that sort of stove. Tobermory has told me that if we get it too hot the steam rises up into the Park and makes a funny smell.' Madame Cholet breathed deeply and added, 'A *funny* smell from my cooking, really, it is very insulting. A delicious smell yes, but not a funny one! However, that is not the point at this moment. If, young Womble,' and Madame Cholet waved a wooden spoon at Bungo, 'you could discover a way in which to get rid of smells then you might win this wonderful Gold Medal

and the rest of the burrow would be able to have hot snacks all through the day and night, eh?'

'Um,' said Bungo and took the delicious smelling buttercup shake to Orinoco.

'I don't think I can manage all of it,' said Orinoco in a very small voice, but somehow with a great effort he did force himself to swallow every single drop before falling back on to his grass-filled pillow. He appeared to be extremely weak but when Bungo in an attempt to cheer him up, told him about Madame Cholet's problems, a faint – a very faint – light of enthusiasm lit up Orinoco's small round eyes.

'You mean we can't have a nice little snack in the middle of the night? Really that's too bad. I sometimes feel exactly like a nice little something if I can't sleep properly. There's nothing like a nice little something to send you off again. Dear me.'

'Well you'll sleep all right now,' said Bungo cheerfully. 'Buttercup shake is just the thing to send you off and tomorrow you'll be right as tenpence.'

'I may be,' Orinoco agreed doubtfully, 'but I shan't bank on it. Diesel paw is a very nasty complaint, you know. Thank you Bungo, old Womble, I shan't forget your kindness . . .'

Bungo tip-toed away feeling rather pleased with himself, but Orinoco, his own front paws folded neatly on his top sheet, continued to gaze up at the roof of the burrow while his brain worked busily.

He had not, of course, been to Great Uncle Bulgaria's little talk that evening, but one way and another he had gathered what it was all about. And to his way of thinking there was only one way to win that Gold Medal, a medal which might well cover the best sort of milk chocolate, and that was to work out the answer to Madame Cholet's little problem.

'Fancy *wanting* to get rid of delicious cooking smells though ...' murmured Orinoco, 'still,' and he licked the last of the buttercup shake off his whiskers, 'still, I suppose it is a sort of smell pollution in a way ... and what Womble is better suited to solve it than me!'

As it happened, quite a few Wombles now began to discover that Great Uncle Bulgaria's latest idea was not just a way of getting them to work harder, for when they came to think it over it was rather like being asked to fight a battle against a big, bad enemy called Pollution. What was more, the Womble who fought the hardest would get a gold medal. And each Womble was soon very certain in his or her own mind that he would be the winner.

Orinoco, slowly recovering his appetite (although still somewhat bald in places) folded his paws over his stomach, shut his eyes tightly and tried to think of ways in which to get rid of those cooking smells – delicious though they might be. When this got too hard for him he thought about the medal and whether he would ask for one that was made of peppermint cream or liquorice toffee.

'Um, um, um,' said Orinoco dreamily and only just stopped himself from scratching.

Tomsk saw the whole matter quite differently. Once he had grasped what it was all about he said simply:

'I shall go for the water.'

'You always do,' said Bungo, who was very busy drawing strange looking diagrams on the back of an ironed out paper-bag. 'You go swimming twice a day now, don't you?'

'No, only once and that's in the mornings. In the evening I go and look at the birds and the fishes and that's why . . .'

'Whatever for? They're such dull animals. You can never get a civil word out of them. All they ever say is "quack" or "bubble bubble" or "ssss". Especially that big swan, he's a terrible "sss"-er.'

'I'm trying to explain, if you'd only listen,' said Tomsk patiently. 'I look at them to make sure they're all right and a lot of them aren't. Some of them are quite poorly. That swan "sssssses" because he's got . . .'

But Bungo had gone back to his drawing so Tomsk, who was used to not being listened to because he spoke so slowly, got to his back paws and padded off for his evening stroll. He knew he wasn't very good at explaining things, but the idea which had settled firmly in his mind was that somehow he was going to keep the water in the Serpentine clear and clean. He was sure that some of his fishy and feathered ac-quaintances were off-colour because of the extraordinary things that kept getting dumped in the water. Why, only yesterday he had duck-dived nose foremost straight into an enormous metal object. He'd seen stars for quite five minutes afterwards and his nose was still sore.

There was a thin moon shining through the dark branches of the trees and the grass was stiff with frost as Tomsk, noiseless as a shadow, made his way to the water's edge. Most of the birds were roosting for the night, but the big swan was sitting grumpily on the path and only turned its long neck and tried rather half-heartedly to hiss – but all that came out of its beak was a noise like 'GURGLE – GURGLE – SLLLLLP'.

'What's the matter then?' asked Tomsk gently, but

keeping well clear at the same time because he knew very well that if the swan turned nasty it would be even stronger than he was.

The swan put back its head, its long neck jerking in the most peculiar manner and then it rose unsteadily to its webbed feet and waddled, in that ungraceful way that swans have when they are out of the water, down to the very edge of the Serpentine and tried to drink. And then to Tomsk's horror and dismay the large bird seemed to flop over so that half its body was under water.

'Swans can't drown,' whispered Tomsk. 'They can't!'

But this one quite obviously was drowning, for it was sinking exactly like a boat which has struck a rock.

'Oh dear, oh lor,' muttered Tomsk, shifting from paw to paw and scratching his head. 'I say swan, don't do that. Come on now, there's a good bird.'

The swan settled a little deeper, sending a ripple of water right up to Tomsk's twitching back paws. Tomsk looked round wildly, hoping that he might see Great Uncle Bulgaria and Tobermory out for their evening stroll. But there was nobody about at all – nobody who would be able to help or advise him that is, for there were still a number of cars swishing over the Serpentine Bridge; but Tomsk's opinion of Human Beings was not very high and, anyway, the Wombles were under strict instructions *not* to get mixed up with them, as it might well lead to a Great Womble Hunt.

'Oh help,' whispered Tomsk and on those words the swan sank out of sight. There were more ripples and a few bubbles rose to the surface.

If it had been Bungo or Orinoco or even possibly Great Uncle Bulgaria standing there, they would have thought the drowning swan a very sad sight, but they would also have known that a swan can be a most ungrateful, stupid and indeed downright dangerous bird. But Tomsk didn't think that far, in fact he didn't think at all, he just obeyed the impulse that came from his kind heart and plunged straight into the cold water in a sort of running dive which brought him into collision with a large, feathery and extremely solid body – and bruised his nose all over again.

'Dratted bird,' said Tomsk and the words came up to the surface as 'Derlum-derlum-derlum-dlllmp', which sent a sleepy shoal of roach flickering off in a wild search for cover. The other fish, being rather brighter in the head, had already shot away after the impact of Tomsk's dive. While a very old carp, who was so old that nothing frightened him any more, actually came slowly out of his retreat to discover what was happening.

'Get off,' said Tomsk (only it came out as 'Derlum-dlllllf') as the carp nudged his elbow. Tomsk was very good at holding his breath under water, but his paws kept sliding off the large feathery yet slippery body and after some minutes of this Tomsk felt his head start buzzing. In desperation he seized hold of the swan's webbed feet and towed it in a most undignified way back to dry land. Something slimy and extremely nasty kept wrapping itself round Tomsk's furiously paddling back paws and, if he hadn't been such a determined Womble, he would have let the swan sink and swum off for dear life. But Tomsk was the kind of creature, who once he had set his paw to something, never let go and so, within a very short space of time he was lugging the half-drowned swan up on to the hard, gritty bank with the curious carp following them every inch of the way.

'Go off. Shoo!' said Tomsk breathlessly and shook himself violently. The slimy, clinging feeling remained round his ankles, however, and the carp continued to gape at him from the water's edge. Tomsk whirled round and round looking over his shoulder, till his heartbeats slowed down as he saw by the light of the moon that it was not some terrible monster which had got its tentacles wrapped round him, but a long piece of slimy material that had become twisted into

a rope. Tomsk unsheathed his claws, got a grip on it and pulled. The greenish-black rope twisted like a snake across the path until it reached the still body of the swan and then the swan, too, jerked. Tomsk paused, his eyes round as buttons and then gave another little pull. Once again the swan moved, not just its head this time, but its curved neck and its feathery body as well.

'Oh lor!' said Tomsk. His fur was all prickly with fright, but he tightened his grip and gave a really strong tug. What happened next was even worse than what had gone before, for the swan spun round and made a dreadful choking sound and at the same instant the rope which had been stuck down its long neck was jerked free. Tomsk went flying backwards and landed with a thud that really did drive all the air out of his lungs this time.

'I'm dead,' thought Tomsk wildly, seeing stars for the second time in twenty-four hours. He struggled and struggled to try and breathe, but nothing happened except that his paws flapped feebly and then, just as it seemed as if Tomsk was going to faint clean away, something very heavy landed on his fat, furry body and began to jump up and down. Suddenly Tomsk's lungs began to work again, the whirling stars vanished and Tomsk opened his eyes and found himself looking directly into two far-apart black eyes and an open yellow beak. Somewhere beyond all this were two enormous flapping wings, but Tomsk was too terrified to take in anything but the fact that the swan had somehow managed to return to life, that it was no longer being suffocated by the slimy rope, and was now bouncing up and down on his, Tomsk's, chest with its not inconsiderable weight.

'Waaaaaaaah,' said Tomsk and then obeyed his instincts. In one lightning fast movement he was up on his back paws and running for dear life with the slimy green rope bobbing along behind him, while the swan half running and half flying brought up the rear with its wings flapping.

'Waaaaaah!' roared Tomsk and fairly threw himself into the bushes and down the path that led to the front door of the burrow. Luckily for him it hadn't yet been bolted up for the night and he was inside the burrow and had his back to the door, his lungs heaving and his fur up on end, within seconds.

'Hallo, hallo ...' said Great Uncle Bulgaria coming into the passage and looking over the top of his spectacles. 'What's all the fuss about? What have you been up to Tomsk?'

Tomsk leant against the door panting heavily and didn't say anything for a while. Great Uncle Bulgaria leant on his stick and waited patiently. He knew very well that it was no good trying to hurry Tomsk.

'I ...' said Tomsk, 'I – there was – it did – I went – it's after me ...'

'So I see,' said Great Uncle Bulgaria placidly. 'A very nice length of rope. No, bless me, it's nothing of the kind,' and he poked at the slimy mess on the floor of the burrow with his stick, 'it's material of some sort. Probably a lace curtain. Dear me I didn't know people still used them. I remember when I was a young Womble and She was Queen ...' Great Uncle Bulgaria's voice took on its reminiscent tone, as it always did when he looked backwards to the days when he had been quite a young Womble in the reign of Queen Victoria, 'why in those days Human Beings *always* had lace curtains. I'd no idea they were still in use. It's a most useful find Tomsk. Dirty and smelly at the moment it may be, but Madame Cholet will soon boil it clean. Off to bed now, it's very late. Or was there something more that you wished to tell me?'

Tomsk stared at Great Uncle Bulgaria, his mind all muddled about the events of the evening. It would take such a long time to explain everything that had happened, and now he came to think about it, he really was very tired. It was all quiet outside the burrow too, so perhaps the swan had gone back to the Serpentine and forgotten all about him.

'No, nothing really,' said Tomsk. 'Nothing important that is. G'night Great Uncle Bulgaria.'

And Tomsk thudded off down the burrow, the slimy curtain wound round his front paws.

Later, a great deal later, he was to regret bitterly his missed opportunity. If only he'd been less sleepy and not so bewildered he would have told Great Uncle Bulgaria the whole story of the swan and the curtain and the carp.

Only he didn't, and that was where Tomsk's troubles really began ...

3   The vanishing tidy-bags

Bungo finished his drawings on the back of the paper-bag, sighed and shook his head. His own private plan for winning the Gold Medal had been to collect more rubbish than anybody else, but he could not work out how he was going to do it. He hadn't done so much real thinking since he was in the Womblegarten and not only had it made his head ache, it had also got him exactly nowhere!

It was all very disappointing when he'd been so certain that he would win and, what was more, he knew exactly what kind of medal he wanted. It would have a picture of him on one side of it and *For Courage in the Face of Battle* on the other.

'Tck, tck, tck,' said Bungo and went in search of Orinoco who was now on light duties.

'You look a bit funny,' said Bungo.

'It's not polite to say so. Lots of Wombles have little bald patches from time to time and my appetite's *much* better. Almost recovered really. Are you working today Bungo?'

'Yes,' said Bungo gloomily. 'And it'll be ever such hard work because there was a high wind in the night and you know what *that* means!'

'Bus tickets, milk cartons, newspapers, paper-bags, carrier-bags, hats, umbrellas, scarves, handkerchiefs, plastic bags, gloves ...'

'There's no need to sound so cheerful about it! And anyway they're all small,' said Bungo.

'Small?' said Orinoco, puzzled.

'*Little* bits of rubbish. Who wants *little* bits? I say Orinoco, old friend, you wouldn't care to lend a paw would you?'

'I can't you know. I would if I could, really, but I'm still on light duties.'

'Gloves and newspapers *are* light.'

'Light duties *inside* the burrow,' said Orinoco rather smugly.

'Ho hum,' said Bungo, his spirits going even further down. He watched Orinoco trundle off down the burrow in the direction of the kitchen and then perked up as he saw the large figure of Tomsk coming out of the library.

'I say Tomsk, old Womble,' said Bungo. 'I've got ever such a busy morning ahead. More than I can manage really, so would you like to help? We could go shares in whatever we find.'

Tomsk looked up at the clock which Tobermory had mended and got going. It had a habit of leaping forwards every ten minutes because Tobermory hadn't been able to make exactly the right spare parts for it. But on the half hour and the hour it was always perfectly correct.

'Sorry,' mumbled Tomsk. 'The sun's up. *It* can see me in the half-light.'

'It?' asked Bungo, curious in spite of his disappointment.

'The ...' said Tomsk and then mumbled something and hurried off with his head down so that he didn't see Tobermory coming out of his Workshop and the two Wombles collided.

'Mind, mind, mind,' said Tobermory holding a metal disc above his head. He glowered at Tomsk and went off in the direction of Great Uncle Bulgaria's room, his forehead creased with concentration. He knocked on the door and both Tomsk and Bungo heard the deep voice of Great Uncle Bulgaria say:

'You can't come in. I'm busy. Very busy indeed. Important business. Writing to *The Times*.'

'If you ask me,' said Bungo to nobody in particular, 'some very odd things are happening in the burrow these days. Things aren't what they used to be at all. Nobody listens to anybody any more. Wombles don't even seem to know other Wombles' names even and ...'

'Hallo Bungo,' said a small voice.

'And ... who – what ... oh it's you, Wellington. What do you want?'

Wellington was the smallest and the most shy of the working Wombles and he spent most of his time in the library. He wore large round spectacles and, although he had shown great bravery in past Womble difficulties, he still couldn't get over the habit of apologizing a lot of the time. He did it now:

'I'm sorry if I disturbed you,' he said. 'I'll go if you're busy ...'

'No, no,' Bungo said quickly, 'I say Wellington, I suppose you wouldn't care to lend me a paw, would you? I'm on early morning duty. Half-shares of course.'

'Half-shares?' said Wellington timidly.

'In whatever we find and clear up.'

'But why should I want half-shares, Bungo?'

'Oh never mind. Will you or won't you come and help me?'

'All right,' said Wellington cheerfully. 'Hold on a tick while I get a tidy-bag from the stores. You know I haven't been out on the Common for months.'

'It's not the Common now, we're in Hyde Park.'

'Oh yes, I keep forgetting. I spend such a lot of time sorting out comics and leaflets and books, let alone newspapers that I ...' said Wellington, and disappeared into Tobermory's Workshop to reappear with an enormous tidy-bag nearly as large as himself. He went on chirpily, 'that I quite often forget that we Wombles have moved our quarters. I'm not very good at clearing-up you know. I get lost so quickly. No sense of direction that's my trouble. It's nice to get out into the fresh air again, isn't it, although I suppose you're used to it. I remember when I travelled across London that time to Buckingham Palace I was astonished at the petrol smells.* London does smell awful, although it's not so bad here in the middle of Hyde Park, especially early in the morning like this – whoops!'

Wellington reeled backwards as the cold wind from the north-west that was whipping across London, caught him fair and square and nearly knocked him off his back paws. Bungo steadied him and the two small Wombles, their ears and their fur brushed out straight behind them, made their rather unsteady way towards Bungo's patch.

All too quickly Bungo saw that his worst fears had been realized. All kinds of rubbish were tangled up in the bushes and round the tree-trunks, while the bottom of Albert Memorial in Kensington Gardens was positively wrapped in newspaper. And yet, as fast as he and Wellington cleared up one patch of ground, more rubbish was borne in on the wind.

'It's hopeless,' muttered Bungo, stuffing litter into his tidy-bag, 'we'll never ever get it cleared and it's all small stuff too . . .'

And at that exact moment he received a stunning blow on his right ear as a large piece of hardboard whizzed past. Bungo reeled back, but Wellington, who had just succeeded in jamming a load of soft-drink tins into his bag, happened to see the hardboard sailing on its way and made a grab for it.

'Hold tight,' wheezed Bungo.

'I am . . . I think . . .'

The two young Wombles unsheathed their claws and took hold of a corner apiece and then, as the wind was

* See *The Wandering Wombles*.

unusually strong, their back paws suddenly lost contact with the ground and willy-nilly they found themselves bounding and then flying through the air.

'I say,' said Wellington between gasps, 'I never thought I'd fly ...'

'Me neither,' replied a breathless Bungo. 'Just hang on, that's all ...'

The wind gave an extra snort and the next moment, their back paws going like furious little pedals, the two horrified Wombles saw, through a red curtain of driving leaves, a long brick wall dead ahead. There are times when even a Womble is forced to let go and this moment happened now. Bungo and Wellington fell to earth with a 'thump-thump ouch-ouch' and the sheet of hardboard, relieved of their weight, rose another foot and neatly skimmed over the wall. There was a second's pause and then an ominous crash of breaking glass.

'Oh,' said Bungo and looked at Wellington who was sitting bolt upright, two enormous wet leaves plastered right across his spectacles.

'I've gone blind,' said Wellington in a quavering voice.

'Tck!'

Bungo stumped across and removed the leaves and hauled the trembling Wellington to his back paws. Wellington shakily took off his smeared specs, wiped them clean and then looked hopefully at Bungo, because Bungo always seemed to know what to do in an emergency.

'We'd better go and see what's happened, I suppose,' said Bungo. 'I hope it's not *too* bad. Come on, there must be a way into that place somewhere . . .'

With great caution the pair of them edged round the wall until they found a curving drive. It was sheltered from the wind, and was somehow rather eerily quiet, and their hearts were thumping painfully as they rounded a bend and saw before them not some mysterious human home, but row after *row* after ROW of enormous greenhouses.

'I didn't know this was here, did you?' whispered Wellington and Bungo shook his head. Of course they hadn't been living under Hyde Park for long, but even so he thought he had explored most of it, and yet here was this secret place almost on the burrow doorstep.

'Lumme!' said Bungo. 'It's huge and – oh!'

'What is it?' Wellington's fur rose so stiffly he almost resembled a kind of hedgehog.

'Do you suppose we broke one of those?'

Bungo jerked his head towards the shining glass roofs and swallowed.

On tip-toe they began to hunt for the runaway piece of hardboard, but their luck had changed for the better for, when they finally did discover it, it was tucked away in a far corner resting on some pieces of glass which had obviously been broken before and then neatly stacked away. Right beside them was a very small, very dilapidated greenhouse with a few empty flower-pots, old tools, oil-cans and sacks dumped inside its open door.

Wellington put his nose inside and sniffed the smell of damp earth and warmth and suddenly, for no particular reason, it reminded him of his cosy, familiar library. Nobody could feel lost or bewildered in a place like this. In fact it was just the sort of place he liked.

'Are you going to stand in there all day with that soppy smile on your face?' demanded Bungo from the doorway. 'Come and give us a paw can't you?'

'Sorry,' said Wellington automatically. 'Only Bungo I don't honestly think we can get the hardboard back to the burrow in this wind. It's quite safe where it is, you know, and as soon as the wind drops I'll come and help you shift it.'

'Oh all right,' grumbled Bungo sulkily. It really was too bad, because that piece of hardboard would be a start in his own plan to win the medal. It was so large it was about equal to picking up at least a dozen old newspapers.

'Cheer up,' said Wellington who was himself in splendid spirits all of a sudden. 'We've got lots of other rubbish . . .' His voice died into silence and the two Wombles stared at each other in consternation. What with the excitement of chasing the hardboard, almost flying with it, nearly losing it and then finding it again, they had completely forgotten their tidy-bags. And to lose a tidy-bag was a pretty dreadful thing to do.

Without another word they turned on their heels and scampered off into the windy Park.

'We dropped them about there, I think . . .' said Bungo.

'No, there . . .'

'Or there . . .'

'Over there?'

Noses to the ground they scampered backwards and forwards, growing more and more desperate, but the tidy-bags seemed to have vanished. It was as though the Park had opened up and swallowed them.

'They must have blown away,' panted Wellington, leaning against the railings that run from north to south at the western side of Kensington Gardens. His tongue was hanging out and his spectacles had misted over, so he took them off to give them another quick clean. As he did so, he had the strangest feeling that he and Bungo were not alone and the fur tingled all the way up and down his back. He jammed the spectacles back on his nose, but there was nobody about except for a man whistling to his dog over by the Round Pond.

'They *couldn't* have blown away,' replied Bungo crossly. 'They were *full* of rubbish.'

Really it was too bad! Everything had gone wrong today and he could see his Gold Medal fading away before his eyes.

'Somebody must have taken them,' Bungo said darkly.

'I *am* sorry, Bungo.'

'Being sorry doesn't help. Come on. I might have known it would happen when you were around,' Bungo went on most unfairly, but he was now thoroughly out of sorts and getting hungry into the bargain, 'if you don't lose yourself then you jolly well make other Wombles lose their tidy-bags. Don't stand there panting, follow me or you'll be the next thing to vanish, I shouldn't wonder!'

'Yes Bungo,' said Wellington sadly. 'I am . . .' and stopped himself just in time as Bungo glared at him. What Bungo had said might not be fair, but there was a grain of truth in it all the same. Whatever he, Wellington, did always seemed to go wrong somehow. Then he remembered that nice, warm, quiet, deserted little greenhouse and his spirits perked up as he began to think about it; so naturally he forgot to look where he was going and, just after they had scuttled across the Serpentine Road and reached the safe cover of the bushes on the other side, one of Wellington's back paws made sudden contact with something which was both hard and sharp. The next moment he was hopping round and round with the bruised back paw grasped in his two front paws.

'What is it NOW!' demanded Bungo, whose own attention had been caught for a second by the extraordinary behaviour of a swan farther down the Serpentine Road. The bird was waddling up and down with its long neck going from side to side exactly as if it was looking for someone.

'Waiting for a person to feed it, I suppose,' muttered Bungo, rubbing his own rumbling stomach. Then he forgot the swan as he saw that Wellington was still doing his hopping dance.

'Ouch, ouch, ouch,' said Wellington. 'Oh my back paw. My poor back paw.'

'Probably hit it on a stone. That'll teach you to look where – I SAY!'

Bungo let out a sound between a yelp and a bellow and darted past Wellington and into the bushes which quivered and then closed behind him. And then quivered again as Bungo's round backview re-emerged, and Wellington forgot his aching paw for a second and limped over to have a closer look at whatever it was.

'There,' said a puffing Bungo, 'that's what you hit your paw on, you great gormless Womble,' only he said it nicely, like a compliment. 'The handle of this mangle. Isn't it *huge*?

I bet nobody else has found such a big bit of rubbish this morning. Of course you found it really ...'

'You can claim it,' said Wellington generously. 'I'll tell you one thing Bungo, *that* won't blow away!'

After all the difficulties and disappointments of the morning this suddenly seemed like a very funny joke and the pair of them rolled over and over on the grass, gasping and wheezing.

'I stood on the *hangle* of a mangle ...' giggled Wellington.

'Or the handle of a *mandle* ...' said Bungo and rolled over again.

After a few minutes, however, they began to wish that the mangle *wasn't* quite so heavy. It was a most difficult object to transport, both because of its weight and its shape, and the handle (or hangle) caught Bungo several buffets behind the ear, before Wellington had the brilliant idea of tying it (the handle, not the ear) firmly in place with his scarf.

When Tobermory was finally confronted with their find he scratched his nose with his screwdriver, shook his head and said:

'Tck, tck, tck. Now why should any Human Being dump a thing like that? I'll never understand them, not if I live to be *two* hundred. It's in perfect working order, or it will be once I've repaired those rollers and cleaned it up a bit and oiled it and got rid of that rusty patch. It'll be just the thing for mangling ...'

'Or mandling,' whispered Bungo to Wellington, who had to stuff his front paw into his mouth to stop himself from laughing.

'For *mangling*,' said Tobermory loudly, 'that lace curtain which Tomsk found. Well you're a silly pair, but you've done well today for once. Now where are your tidy-bags?'

At this all the laughter vanished from the faces of Bungo and Wellington. Indeed their faces got longer and longer as Tobermory told them extremely firmly what he thought of young Wombles who were not only silly, but forgetful, careless and irresponsible as well.

'We have never, EVER lost a tidy-bag before,' said Tobermory. 'Let alone TWO tidy-bags. I've got a good mind to take you off outside work for a week and to send you back to the Womblegarten where Miss Adelaide can keep an eye on you.'

Wellington shut his eyes tightly at the dreadfulness of this threat and Bungo sagged at the knees.

'However,' said Tobermory, 'I shan't. Not because you don't deserve it, but because we need every working Womble we can lay our paws on if we're to make a success of Womble Conservation Year.'

As neither Bungo nor Wellington could think of anything to say to this they wisely kept silent and Tobermory sent them off to breakfast with a further, 'Tck, tck, tck!'

He had problems enough of his own without having more

dumped in his lap. His own particular idea wasn't going well, the high wind had brought a great deal of dust into the burrow, and now he'd have to ask Miss Adelaide to get her small Wombles to make two more tidy-bags in their next paw-craft lesson ...

But as it happened Tobermory had to do no such thing. For when Tomsk drew back the bolts on the front door of the burrow the following morning he found, sitting on the ground outside, two neatly packed tidy-bags. And pinned to one of them was a scrap of paper which read,

'Greetings. ow.'

A shiver ran right through Tobermory's silky grey fur.

4   Chewy-crunchy-chocky

'Ow!' said Great Uncle Bulgaria with a snort. 'What kind of a name is *that* I should like to know? Still the whole business is most mysterious, Tobermory, and I don't mind telling you I don't like it. I don't like it *at all*. It's all a bit too close to home for comfort. How did this ow person know where we live? How did he know the tidy-bags belonged to us? Drat that Bungo. Trust him, of all Wombles, to get us into a mess like this ...'

'He *did* find the mandle – er mangle,' said Tobermory, 'it's a splendid piece of Victoriana. I remember when I was young ...'

'Yes, yes, yes. I remember too. Great Aunt Thessaly had one in the Wimbledon burrow. But let's stick to the point, old friend. We'd better double the Day Watch Womble guard just in case there is any sort of trouble. We don't want one of Them' (by which Great Uncle Bulgaria meant Human Beings) 'to come ferreting round after us. Think what happened to Cousin Yellowstone!'*

'Ho hum,' agreed Tobermory and for a moment the two old Wombles recalled the fur-raising adventures of Yellowstone who had been captured nearly sixty years ago, but who had managed to escape and had then travelled all round the world until he settled down to become the Patriarch of the American Wombles.

'Nice chap, Yellowstone,' said Great Uncle Bulgaria, suddenly not sticking to the point at all. 'Hope he'll come and

* See *The Wombles*.

see us again one day. Which reminds me, did my letter to *The Times* go off all right?'

'Posted last night. It was Yellowstone who told me about making a deep-freeze. A most useful machine it's turned out to be too. Now that winter is coming on we shan't have to worry about being short of food. Madame Cholet says . . .'

'Yes, yes, yes,' Great Uncle Bulgaria stilled his rocking-chair and tapped on the floor with his stick. 'But as I was saying, old friend, we shall have to be very careful in the future and I'd like a word with young Bungo. Atchoo!'

'You can't. Not at the moment. He went out early. He's got one of his keen spells on. Catching a cold?'

'No. It's this confounded dust. I wish you'd do something about it, Tobermory.'

'I had thought of rigging up that curtain Tomsk brought in, but the difficulty is the dust is coming *down* from the roof as much as *in* from the door. I'll send Bungo along as soon as he returns. He'd gone off with Wellington, both of 'em looking as though they were up to something. And I'll tell you something odd . . .'

'I'll tell *you* something,' interrupted Great Uncle Bulgaria, leaning forward and putting his chin on his stick, 'I've got an *odd* feeling. Had it for some time too. I feel uneasy.'

'Oh?'

'I may be old, but I've still got all my Womble instincts,' said Great Uncle Bulgaria slowly, 'and I feel that we're being *watched*!'

'Them?' asked Tobermory after a long pause.

Slowly Great Uncle Bulgaria shook his white head and then felt for his purple handkerchief as a faint eddy of dust swirled down.

'Human Beings? I don't know,' he said thickly through the handkerchief, 'wish I did. Drat, here it comes again. At-ishoooo.'

The something odd which Tobermory had been about to

mention was the behaviour of Wellington, who at this particular moment was helping Bungo to carry the sheet of
hardboard away from the greenhouses. The wind had
dropped as suddenly as it had arisen and it had started to
rain.

'I can manage,' puffed Bungo, who had his tidy-bag slung
round his neck, 'it's not heavy, only *big*. Shift it onto my
back.'

Wellington did as he was asked and Bungo lurched forwards, looking for all the world like an enormous square
mushroom with a short fat stalk.

'I can carry it on my own, you know,' said Bungo.
'Perhaps you might like to follow me.'

'No thank you, Bungo,' Wellington replied surprisingly, 'I
want to stay here.'

'You'll get lost,' said Bungo, addressing his own back paws
as he was unable to straighten up, or even to turn round,
because he was frightened he might hit something with his
awkward load.

'No, I shan't,' said Wellington even more surprisingly, 'I
borrowed a compass from Tobermory in the stores this
morning and I've got . . .' and then he stopped.

'Well, be careful,' said Bungo, who had other things on his

mind, 'see you back at the burrow. Don't let anybody catch you!'

He meant it as a joke, but Wellington was suddenly reminded of that weird feeling he'd had yesterday that somebody or something was watching him and shivered. Then he forgot all about it as he turned back to the little deserted greenhouse, shut the door behind him and put the compass down on the wooden slats of the bench. Next, he drew out a tattered little booklet which he put beside the compass. And then he breathed a great big sigh of happiness.

The title of the booklet was *Plant Pollution*.

Wellington had found his own particular idea.

He propped his chin in both front paws and began to read.

Bungo's journey back to the burrow followed a somewhat zig-zag path and, had he but known it, a startled early morning motorist driving across the bridge over the Serpentine, thought for a moment that he must have gone quite mad. After all, Human Beings do not expect to see at six o'clock in the morning a sheet of hardboard with small furry legs. The motorist drew into the side of the road and mopped his forehead and then his eyes grew even rounder because, in spite of the early morning mist, he was quite certain that he could see a swan walking up and down like a sentry with rows and rows of fish watching its progress, their heads turning from right to left as they did so.

The motorist took a deep breath and drove on, leaving behind him a very nasty smell of petrol fumes. Which was something he *didn't* notice, as he was used to them.

During the next twenty minutes Bungo felt very important as he presented the hardboard to Tobermory and then not important at all, in fact almost humble, while Great Uncle Bulgaria had a few words with him. He was still in a most unusually subdued mood when he was collared by Orinoco.

'You look as if you've got a touch of the diesel paw,' said
Orinoco.

'Well I haven't.'

'You're just the Womble I wanted to see, anyway. Come
and lend us a paw.'

'Can't, I . . .' said Bungo and then with a great sigh recalled
the last stinging words of Great Uncle Bulgaria. 'We're all in
this together, young Womble. We work together as a
burrow. All for one and one for all. We're not after indi-
vidual glory, although I don't suppose for one moment
you're clever enough to know what I mean. If we're going to
fight pollution we must do it together. In the Park, in the
streets . . . oh get on and get out and start tidying up, do!'

'O.K.,' said Bungo. 'It was a lovely piece of hardboard,
too. Anyway, I thought you were on light duties.'

'*Very light*,' agreed Orinoco, 'but outside the burrow this
time. Tobermory says that a lot of schoolchildren were in
the Park yesterday on a nature ramble, whatever *that* is, and
– of course – being Human Beings they didn't bother to use
all the litter bins. I'm hungry again.'

'You always are now you're better,' said Bungo gloomily.
'I'll get my tidy-bag.'

'And a prodder,' Orinoco called after him.

So a few minutes later they checked out with Tomsk and began work. It was the stickiest work that either of them had ever had to do, for in spite of the drizzle they kept getting stuck. Stuck not with good old-fashioned mud, but with toffee papers and sweet wrappers and paper-bags.

'Yuk,' said Orinoco, struggling to get his back paws out of the gummy mess.

'Drat the thing,' muttered Bungo, trying to peel a piece of wrapping with the words 'Best Ramsgate Rock' off his chest. Only the more he pawed at it, the more stuck it became.

'Oh dear, oh dear,' muttered Orinoco, stumping up and down, 'oh it does hurt . . .'

'What does? . . . get *off*! . . . What does!'

'Reading all the lovely words. Listen to this Bungo . . .' Orinoco lifted up his back paw and craned his head over his shoulder, squinting slightly, ' "Yum-yum toffees melt in the mouth." '

' "Ramsgate rock is chewy all-through," ' said Bungo, peering down at his fur-spattered paper.

' "Raspberry lollipops roll round the tongue . . ." '

' "Chumpy-chocs are good for you . . ." '

'They're not at all good for *me*,' Orinoco said furiously, as he jumped up and down with a dreadful sucking noise. 'Lend me your prodder, Bungo.'

Bungo passed across what had once been an umbrella before Tobermory had adapted it to a sharp-pointed stick, rather like the kind that Park Keepers carry. Orinoco did what he could with it, his own now being stuck fast up to the hilt with sweet papers, but he was unable to free his back paws, so in the end he gave it up as a bad job and clumped off looking as though he was wearing very thick-soled shoes.

Bungo was just about winning his own particular fight with the wrappers that had been glued to his chest, when the

wind sighed softly and a swirl of toffee papers descended on him.

'Get off, *off*, OFF,' said Bungo, flapping his paws as though at a swarm of bees. The wind obligingly died away and more toffee papers fluttered down.

'Hee hee, ho hum, you look . . .' chortled Orinoco and then stopped, quite literally struck dumb as a piece of gooey plastic paper settled round his mouth. He licked it, rolling his eyes, and then tried to free himself – only both front paws got stuck and quite a lot of his newly grown fur had been painfully removed before he was able to breathe again properly.

By the time Bungo and Orinoco had cleared up all the mess they looked as if they had been in the wars and Tomsk, who had been peering round the door of the burrow in a very nervous way which was most unlike him, opened his mouth in astonishment at this odd sight. Then his face wrinkled up and he went, 'Ah-ah-ah-AH-ATISHOOOOOOO!'

'It's the dust,' said Tobermory coming out of his Workshop, 'there's been a lot coming down from . . . good gracious goodness me!' And Tobermory suddenly lost his usual stern expression and slapped his knees and rocked backwards and forwards and went, 'Ho ho ho ho hum . . .'

'It's not funny,' growled Orinoco, slapping in quite a different way at the maddening scraps of paper that were still sticking to his fur.

'Not funny at all,' barked Bungo, slapping and grabbing and scratching all at the same time.

'Ho ho ho ho hum, of course it isn't,' said Tobermory rubbing the back of a paw across his eyes.

'Ho, ho, ho . . .' rumbed Tomsk. 'Atishooooo.'

As Tomsk was such a large Womble it was a particularly powerful sneeze, powerful enough to act like a kind of miniature whirlwind inside the burrow and to blow the less firmly attached sweet papers off Bungo and Orinoco and to send them up to the ceiling where they stuck.

'Bless you,' said Tobermory as Tomsk rubbed his streaming eyes. 'No, you're quite right young Bungo, it isn't funny really. Well, at least not from *your* point of view. You'd better go and ask Madame Cholet to put some kettles on the stove – if it's still hot – so that you can have a warm wash down. We don't want any more cases of falling fur. Leave your prodders here and I'll see what I can do with them. What a very nasty gooey mess to be sure.'

Bungo and Orinoco were half-way down the burrow when Tobermory, who was staring absentmindedly at the toffee papers on the ceiling, called after them:

'And by the by, Bungo, that hardboard you brought in has proved to be most useful. Great Uncle Bulgaria and I have turned it into a Womble gold star chart.'

'What's that, Tobermory?'

'Mmmmm?'

Tobermory was now revolving slowly on his back paws with his gaze fixed on the ceiling. He poked at it with one of the prodders and then turned and hurried off to his Workshop, to return a moment later with a wooden crate under one arm and a bucket and brush under the other.

'What's a Womble gold star chart?'

'It shows how much rubbish each working Womble has collected while on duty. I weigh and measure the rubbish and then allot a gold star. You're ahead at the moment, Bungo, because of your mangle. Tomsk is just behind you, though. Um. Yes. Hold on.'

'You told us to go and have a wash and then breakfast!' said Orinoco on a rising note.

'Breakfast,' said Tobermory crossly, 'don't you ever think of anything but food?'

'Not often,' said Orinoco truthfully, 'and at this *particular* moment I'm thinking about it *particularly* hard. It was finding all those sweet papers that . . .'

'Exactly and precisely,' said Tobermory, climbing down off the box and beaming at Orinoco in a way which made that young Womble feel most uneasy. 'Come back here, you two. I've got a little job for you.'

'Now?' said Bungo in a small voice.

'Now! As you're good and sticky already, a little more stickiness won't hurt you. You can paper up the cracks in the ceiling with all those sweet wrappers. They're just what we wanted.'

'Oh Tobermory do we have to?' wailed Orinoco. 'They've got all those lovely words on them. Chewy, crunchy, chocky – and I really am *ever* so hungry. I haven't been well, you know, and . . .'

'*Now*,' said Tobermory in a voice that meant 'Now, This Very Minute'.

Five minutes later he put his head round the Workshop door to see how matters were progressing. Bungo was standing on the box using the brush to stick the sweet papers firmly into place, and Orinoco was dipping the next lot of papers into the bucket of paste before handing them up to his fellow Womble. Both of them now looked as if they had been out in a snow-storm.

'Good work,' said Tobermory, 'I'll mark it up on the Womble star chart. Who knows, one of you might win the Gold Medal because of this.'

The door closed softly and Orinoco groaned deeply as he dipped the paper from a chocolate bar into the bucket and then handed it to Bungo.

'Oh shut up, do,' grunted Bungo. 'I'm just as hungry as you are. If not hungrier.'

'It's not that,' sighed Orinoco, reaching for another sweet paper, 'well not *just* that. It's reading all those lovely words. Every time I walk down the burrow from now on I shall only have to look up and I'll see "chewy – crunchy – chocky" written all over the ceiling. And it won't matter if

I've just had breakfast or lunch or tea, I shall start feeling hungry at once. I know I shall. I wish I'd never *heard* of light duties!'

5 Things that go 'woooo' in the night

Winter came early and with a hard snap that iced over the Serpentine and covered the whole of the Park and Kensington Gardens with white frost. The Wombles, who unless they are as old as Great Uncle Bulgaria, don't feel the cold, thoroughly enjoyed the seasonable weather. Nearly all of them were now deeply involved in what was mysteriously called 'Womble Conservation Year', which to them meant who had the most gold stars on the chart. At this particular moment Bungo was slightly ahead of Orinoco, while Tomsk was lagging behind (he'd been getting more and more odd recently) and Wellington was nowhere at all.

If there was a strange fidgety feeling among the older Wombles, the younger ones didn't notice it, because they were so wrapped up in the contest.

'It's all very well for them,' said Madame Cholet quite crossly for her, for normally she was the most good-natured and easy-going of Wombles, 'they know they won't go short of food because of my deep-freeze. But how am I supposed to produce *hot* meals when Tobermory orders me to run my stove only eight hours out of the twenty-four. Answer me that, eh?'

'Ah,' said Miss Adelaide to whom this question was addressed. 'It *is* a problem, I quite see that. But then we all have them,' and she crossed her silky grey paws on the lap of her starched apron and sighed softly.

Madame Cholet, who had been polishing up her saucepans so that they shone like silver, looked sharply across the burrow at her old friend.

The Womble kitchen-cum-workroom was always a very comfortable part of the Hyde Park burrow. It had an old-fashioned stove at one end, while screwed to the ceiling was what had once been a spring mattress. Thanks to Tobermory's skilful paws it had been transformed into a series of hooks from which hung all kinds of pots and pans and ladles, all of which had been reclaimed from the rubbish dump, from bushes and even from the Serpentine and the Round Pond. Now, repaired and cleaned they were the joy of Madame Cholet's heart. Like the rest of the Wombles she could never understand why Human Beings didn't take more care of, or pride in, their belongings.

There was also a long scrubbed table made out of once-upon-a-time dumped crates, two large cupboards which had once been a wardrobe, a filing cabinet and a couple of chairs. Miss Adelaide was sitting in the one made of re-inforced cane, while Madame Cholet had inserted her portly form into what a Human Being might have called an old tin bath. Only now it was suspended from the spring mattress by ropes and was lined with pieces of foam rubber and furthermore, as Madame Cholet knew very well, was just about the most restful seat ever invented.

'Go on, Adelaide,' said Madame Cholet, just touching the floor with her back paws so that her seat-cum-swing rocked delightfully.

'That's it, I wish I could,' said Miss Adelaide as she reached down to the painted plastic bucket at her side and brought out the remains of a scarlet sweater which she began to unravel. 'My little Wombles are so keen to take part in the contest and to fight pollution – I've drawn it as a great big giant, on the Womblegarten blackboard and we've called it Pollu for short – but there's not much I can give them to do. We repair things and we make tidy-bags and we pulp old

newspapers and magazines and make them into useful objects, but they need *more* than that. And, what's more – and this is just between you and me – I've noticed a certain restlessness in them recently. They're uneasy. I'm not a particularly fanciful Womble, but . . .'

'But,' nodded Madame Cholet, 'do not disturb yourself, Adelaide, I have felt it too. Even while I have been cooking – when Tobermory *allows* me to have my stove going I may add – I have felt this creeping in my fur. Someone is spying on us. Who or what it is I don't know, but it is *there*, I agree with you Adelaide. There is an odd feeling in this burrow altogether and I don't like it.'

'I have sometimes wondered,' said Miss Adelaide, and then stopped short, her silky paws moving faster than ever as she began to wind the scarlet wool round and round a piece of cardboard which had been cut from the back of a food packet.

'Continuez,' said Madame Cholet who, since she had a French name, liked to speak a bit of the language sometimes.

'Well I am interested in history as you know, but although I have searched most carefully through Great-Great-Great-Uncle Hohenzollern's *Womble History of the World* I cannot discover any clue as to why this very spacious and beautiful burrow was suddenly deserted by the Wombles who built it all those hundreds of years ago. And it has occurred to me, Madame Cholet, that . . .'

Miss Adelaide's paws were now a perfect blur of movement while Madame Cholet was almost falling out of her chair with curiosity. Miss Adelaide cleared her throat and went on in a low, hurried voice, 'That perhaps the burrow is – is haunted?'

'Tiens!' said Madame Cholet and threw her apron over her head.

'Now don't take on,' said Miss Adelaide rather crossly and

already regretting that she had said so much. She had forgotten how excitable her old friend could be sometimes and, when at last Madame Cholet removed the apron and her chair had stopped going round and round, and she had had a little sip of elm bark juice to steady her nerves, Miss Adelaide said in the voice that she used for small fidgety Wombles in the back row of the classroom:

'Now listen to me, please. It was only an idea of mine. A very foolish idea as I now realize. You must put it out of your head completely and not one word of what I have been saying must go beyond these four walls. We don't want to start any silly rumours, do we?'

Madame Cholet shook her head and had another sip, her paw still a bit on the shaky side.

Had she but known it Miss Adelaide's warning was already too late, for it so happened that Orinoco was outside the door at this exact moment. The kitchen-workroom was quite his favourite place in the burrow and anyway he had been planning to have another look at that stove. Orinoco stood as one rooted to the spot, his paw raised to knock on the door.

His teeth chattered in his head, he gave a little whimper and then rushed off in search of Bungo. But Bungo was being very busy and important in the Workshop, helping – or so he said – Tobermory to sort through the day's rubbish. And of course to weigh it up. He'd brought in a bent iron chair that morning and it had put him well ahead in stars, so that he could now visualize the Gold Medal, the presentation and the modest speech he would make, quite clearly.

'But this is important,' hissed Orinoco from the doorway.

'So is this . . .'

'If you're looking for a job, Orinoco . . .' said Tobermory.

Orinoco slid backwards and gently shut the door behind

him. It was funny the way some of the older members of the burrow seemed to think that the younger members ought to work *all* the time. Especially when this particular younger member had been hard at it for three hours earlier in the day.

Orinoco shook his head over this mystery and went searching for Wellington whom he soon discovered in the library. It was rather a good library, as Human Beings are even more careless with books than they are with most of their belongings, with the result that the shelves were crammed with volumes, ranging from the *Beginning To Read* series to *Zoology 'A' Level to Phd*, whatever *that* meant.

'Pssst!' said Orinoco.

Wellington, who was sitting at a table littered with books and leaflets and papers and coloured felt-tipped pens, had his paws over his ears so naturally enough he didn't hear. He was whispering to himself:

' "... these lead based sprays can be extremely harmful to plant life and ultimately to animal and human existence..." '

'Oi!' shouted Orinoco.

Wellington heard that all right and nearly jumped out of

his fur. Normally the most meek and mild of Wombles he now said furiously:

'Don't DO that. And please go away, I'm awfully busy.'

'Why are you wearing a white coat?' asked Orinoco, not obeying this request at all, but coming farther into the room.

Wellington glanced down at his beautifully mended jacket, which once upon a time might have belonged to a waiter before it had been thrown over the railings in Kensington Gardens. It was rather on the large size for him. He said:

'I'm being a scientist. I don't know why they have to wear white coats, but they all do in the pictures I've seen. *Please* go away.'

'Don't you want to hear what I've got to tell you? It's ever so important.'

'No, thank you.'

'Then I shan't tell you. The burrow's haunted, that's all. Still, if you don't want to know about it, I'll go. Only just be careful that something doesn't come woooooing up on you out of the shadows.'

Orinoco said this so well that he frightened himself and two sets of teeth started chattering, before Wellington managed to say in a whisper:

'As a scientist I don't believe in ghosts. But as a Womble I jolly well do. Only, Orinoco, how do you know?'

'That's a secret.' Orinoco laid one paw against his nose and winked.

'Yes, but,' said Wellington glancing nervously over his shoulder, 'it's not exactly the burrow that's haunted. It's *outside* in the Park. Promise you won't split if I tell you something?'

Orinoco shook his head and then glanced over his shoulder. It's odd how, once you start to feel creepy, it grows and grows.

'Well, you know I'm doing sort of secret work on my Pollu idea in that little greenhouse? When I'm inside it I feel as safe as burrows, but when I walk back across the Park I get this feeling that I'm being watched. It takes quite a lot of nerve actually to make myself go there every day.'

Orinoco swallowed and said in an even smaller voice:

'Have you – have you ever seen IT ?'

'Never. But I've felt it very close to me . . .'

They stared at each other, their teeth chattering harder than ever.

'If we tell Great Uncle Bulgaria he'll only tell us not to be silly young Wombles and if we tell Tobermory he'll say the same,' said Orinoco who was now sitting beside Wellington at the table just in case IT should chance to come into the burrow and round the library door.

'What shall we do then?' asked Wellington.

'Tell Tomsk. He's not afraid of anything. Perhaps he'll chase it away . . .'

But Tomsk, when appealed to, only made matters much worse by staring at them stolidly for some while and then saying slowly:

'So *you've* noticed it, have you? I don't like it at all. It follows me around all the time. But don't worry, I won't let it into the burrow if I can possibly help it. I suppose it may have slipped in one day when I wasn't on duty. Oh dear, oh dear.'

Wellington and Orinoco stared at him, for once in their young lives quite unable to speak for several minutes until Orinoco said faintly:

'You mean – you mean you've actually seen IT! What does IT look like?'

'Well what do you suppose it looks like?' snapped Tomsk, who was tired and wet and muddy. 'It's white and its got a long neck and it's about my size . . .'

And he stumped off leaving Wellington and Orinoco trem-

bling like a couple of jellies. After that, of course, the rumour was all round the burrow in a couple of shakes and a number of very small Wombles started having nightmares and asking for the lights to be left on all night, and even Bungo, who was always boasting how brave he was, kept peering over his shoulder.

'What's the *matter* with them?' demanded Great Uncle Bulgaria. 'They're all behaving like a burrow of idiots instead of sensible Wombles. Ghosts indeed! I never heard such rubbish!'

But all the same he couldn't quite stop himself from drawing his tartan shawl more closely round his shoulders.

'I can't exactly lay my paw on the trouble,' said Tobermory. '*I* know it's nonsense and *you* know it's nonsense, but it's giving the whole burrow an uneasy atmosphere and it's affecting everyone . . .'

'Madame Cholet and Miss Adelaide still not on good terms?' asked Great Uncle Bulgaria, who missed very little on the whole.

Tobermory shook his head and Great Uncle Bulgaria shook out his *Times* and turned to the back page. He brightened visibly as he said:

'There's another in today.'

'Another what?'

'Answer to my advertisement. That was money well spent. But how are things going with you old friend?'

'Ticking over, heh, heh, heh,' said Tobermory, uttering a wheezing sound which was his way of enjoying a private joke. 'Well, back to the Workshop. I'll be glad when this winter's over. There'll be an extra hard frost tonight, I shouldn't wonder, and if it snows as well, the working parties won't be able to go out because of leaving paw-marks. And *that*'ll mean extra work later on and meanwhile we shall all be cooped up indoors and the Silly Ones'll get more jittery than ever.'

'Who's ahead on the chart?'

'Bungo.'

'Trust him,' said Great Uncle Bulgaria and returned to his *Times*.

There was indeed a very hard frost in the night and at dawn, when the temperature rose a little, there was a slight fall of snow. It turned Hyde Park and Kensington Gardens into a glittering white expanse of undulating beauty, but only Tomsk was there to admire it. He knew he wasn't supposed to work under these weather conditions and he very rarely, if ever, disobeyed orders, but there was something he had to do and do quickly if he was to save literally thousands of lives . . .

The sky was still dark when he marked himself out in the book and slid out of the burrow. He slid because strapped to his pack paws were two old tennis rackets which he hoped would both disguise his Womble tracks and make it easier for him to move fast. And these days he had to move very fast indeed if he wanted to keep clear of IT. Over his shoulder was an enormous old pickaxe.

'Shoosh-shoosh,' went Tomsk's home-made snowshoes and suddenly he forgot all his immediate worries, because within a very few seconds he found that, if he shuffled along

rather than walking properly, he could slide over the snow quite fast instead of sinking into it.

'Shoosh-shoosh-shoosh.'

Tomsk used the handle of the pickaxe like an Alpine stick and picked up more speed still, his breath hanging in little puffs in the frosty air while his eyes were firmly fixed on the Serpentine.

Yes, just as he'd feared, it was covered in thick slippery ice. He knew that the early morning bathers would be down later on, but by then the roach, perch, ruff, tench, carp, rudd, gudgeon, goldfish, pike and eels who lived in the water, might all be suffocated . . .

So intent was Tomsk on his objective that he failed to notice that his progress was being watched by two sets of eyes . . .

'PEER-LONK!'

A mallard duck came in to land, skidded and then whizzed along the ice on its rump in a most undignified manner.

Tomsk grinned, slid on to the ice himself, chose a good spot and heaved the pickaxe downwards. The ice was thicker than he'd bargained for and the pickaxe vibrated 'dong-dong-dong' so that Tomsk jittered up and down. But he was not a Womble to give up easily, so he skated further along looking for a more likely spot. When he found it – the ice here had a more grey-than-white appearance – he swung again and this time there was a satisfying 'Creeeeeeeek – CRACK' and a zig-zag pattern of cracks appeared under his feet.

'Once again,' muttered Tomsk and swung mightily.

At the same instant two voices rang out across the silent frosty Park:

'Hooooo Hooooo.'

'Niet!'

Tomsk leapt backwards, losing his snow-shoes as he did so, and the pickaxe went over his shoulder, hit the ice with a ringing tone and then slid away, spinning round and round until it banged into the bank.

But, although Tomsk's reflexes were very good, he had left it too late; there was another tremendous 'creek-creekcrack' and then the ice gave under him and he was tumbled headlong into the dark cold waters of the Serpentine, while the ice crumbled and then began to reform over the black gap.

A line of bubbles rose slowly to the surface, but there was no further sign of Tomsk . . .

Thin ice

Great Uncle Bulgaria got stiffly to his back paws and went over to his study door and opened it, looking up and down the burrow. He shivered and then, drawing his shawl more tightly round his white fur, padded along to the main door.

Yes – exactly as he'd thought! Some careless young Womble had left it wide open, so it was no wonder that the temperature had dropped suddenly. He'd have to call a meeting after breakfast and give them all a talking to. Make a little speech in fact . . .

And then Great Uncle Bulgaria's bright old eyes narrowed, and he looked over and then through both his pairs of spectacles at the trodden snow by the burrow entrance. He muttered 'ho hum' under his breath and turned and picked up the large Duty Book. He read aloud.

'Name of Womble: Tomsk. Tidying area: Serpentine. Time of Departure: 5.31 a.m.'

Then he glanced up at the clock which gave one of its sudden jumps to show that the correct hour was six exactly.

'Not like Tomsk to be lax about shutting the door,' said Great Uncle Bulgaria softly. 'He may be slow, but he's always *careful*. Unlike some I could mention! And what's more . . .'

The old Womble turned his attention once more to the marks in the snow. Now *that* was odd! Very odd indeed . . .

Less than two minutes later a still sleepy-eyed Tobermory,

and an extremely sleepy-eyed Bungo, Orinoco and Wellington were lined up in front of Great Uncle Bulgaria, who was shrugging himself into a white nylon fur coat while he edged his back paws into large boots.

'Now listen to me,' he said. 'I don't wish to alarm any of you, but I *am* worried about Tomsk. He went down to the Serpentine – strictly against my instructions but I'll deal with that side of things later – just over half an hour ago. I don't know what he was up to, but ice is treacherous stuff and that's a large stretch of water . . .'

'Forty-nine point three acres,' said Wellington before he could stop himself and added hurriedly, 'sorry . . .'

'Mm, mm,' said Great Uncle Bulgaria not unkindly. 'Indeed? Well Wombles, these are your instructions . . . Tobermory, I want a stout length of rope and a ladder from the Workshop.'

'Right,' said Tobermory and hurried away.

'Orinoco, you're a fine figure of a Womble again and a little exercise won't hurt *you*. Bungo, you're always telling us how daring you are. Ho hum. Yes! Wellington, you go and turn on the stove and start brewing up some hot, really hot and steaming mind, acorn broth.'

'Yes, Great Uncle Bulgaria,' said Wellington with a ghost

of a sigh. All right, so he wasn't as strong or as round and brave as Bungo (or even Orinoco come to that), but wasn't he going to be allowed to be a real part of this adventure? Particularly when Tomsk had always been a very close friend.

'And then,' said Great Uncle Bulgaria, leaning forward on his stick, 'I want you to go to the library, Wellington, and to bring me that booklet called *Waterways of the Royal Parks*. That's very *very* important and I shall need it down by the Serpentine. Understand?'

'*Rather*!' said Wellington and was away like an arrow.

The sky was still dark, but growing just a shade lighter by the time Great Uncle Bulgaria, sliding slightly in his boots, led his rescue team across the Park to the water's edge. Inside himself he was very worried indeed, but his face and his voice were quite calm as he said:

'Ah yes, just as I thought. Tomsk's tracks are not difficult to follow.'

'And not only Tomsk's,' Tobermory muttered, a deep frown between his bristling grey eyebrows.

'Quite, quite. So Tomsk crossed the ice here and then attacked it, dear me, he *is* a strong young Womble, he made quite a dent I see. And then he went on underneath the bridge and striking northwards. Stop!'

Straight in front of them, where they had obviously been thrown off in a hurry, were Tomsk's snow-shoes. Everybody came to a somewhat slithery halt, especially Tobermory who had a coil of rope over one shoulder and a ladder slung across the other. Bungo caught hold of Tobermory's apron strings and for a moment they skittered round each other.

'Thanks,' said Tobermory, puffing. 'Here, young Bungo, you take the rope. Orinoco, grab hold of the other end of this dratted ladder.'

Behind them came the sound of racing pawsteps and

Wellington came zooming across the ice and then braked by throwing himself sideways in a smooth way that made Bungo blink. He'd never thought of Wellington as being the athletic type of Womble, which only went to show that Bungo didn't know half as much as he thought he did.

'The *Waterways* booklet, Great Uncle Bulgaria,' said Wellington and handed it over.

Great Uncle Bulgaria grunted his thanks and moved forward cautiously, feeling the ice quiver under his boots. It was even worse than he had feared it would be. That great gormless Tomsk had shattered the ice in all directions!

'Put the ladder down flat,' said Great Uncle Bulgaria calmly. 'Orinoco, fasten this rope round your middle, then allow a couple of feet and then Bungo you do the same. Then down on your fronts and crawl along the ladder until I tell you to stop. Now then, what does the booklet say . . .? "It is now found that generally storm water and surface drainage, together with spring water, are sufficient to keep the water in the Round Pond and the Serpentine at a good level, but in an emergency – such as drought or icing – water

is pumped from Duck Island, St James' Park, to the reservoir in Hyde Park . . ." Ho hum. Not much help there. Very well, young Wombles, carry on crawling along the ladder.'

'Please, Great Uncle Bulgaria,' said the somewhat breathless voice of Orinoco in the darkness, 'I've reached a big hole in the ice.'

'Then take a deep breath and go down it. A DEEP breath Orinoco.'

'Yes,' said Orinoco and did as he was told.

It was very cold and murky under the ice and he was not particularly brave and had never pretended to be so, but he had the comforting feel of the rope round his middle and he was very fond of old Tomsk. So Orinoco obediently swam around and when he felt the line tighten and then go slack and a distant splashing sound reached his ears, and he knew that Bungo had joined him, he struck out even further. A big fishy face came out of the gloom and Orinoco waved his paws at it and the old carp moved off, but not very far for it then turned its attention towards Bungo and nudged him on the elbow.

'Get off,' said Bungo.

'Glump, glump, glump,' said the bubbles on the surface.

'Silly young Womble, using up his breath,' muttered Great Uncle Bulgaria who was now lying on the ladder behind Tobermory with Wellington just behind him.

They strained their ears listening for any further sounds. but there was only the steady 'slurp slurp' of the cold water and a very faint creaking noise which slowly grew louder. Wellington glanced over his shoulder and gulped as he saw a large white figure go flying past them. He shut his little eyes tightly and when he opened them again the figure had vanished into the darkness.

'Can't let 'em stay down any longer,' muttered Great Uncle Bulgaria, peering at his watch. 'They've been under a

good ten minutes already! They might freeze stiff as boards
... All right Tobermory. One, two, three – HEAVE!'

It wasn't an easy thing to do, to pull on the rope while
remaining safely on the ladder, and, what made it even more
difficult, was the way in which the ice began to bend under
them so that little rivulets of freezing water lapped against
their fur and, in the case of Great Uncle Bulgaria, trickled
inside his white nylon fur coat.

'HEAVE,' commanded the old Womble, taking no notice
of his discomfort, 'and HEAVE ...'

In some mysterious way Bungo and Orinoco seemed to
have become extremely heavy and Great Uncle Bulgaria,
Tobermory and Wellington were gasping and blowing, and
the ice was starting to crack, when at long last two heads
appeared above the water.

'Pooooof,' said Bungo weakly, for once unable to speak.

'Any sign of Tomsk?' demanded Great Uncle Bulgaria sharply.

Bungo and Orinoco shook their heads and then Orinoco said in a faint voice:

'No, nothing. He's vanished clean away. I'm awfully sorry. Shall we go down again?'

Great Uncle Bulgaria looked at their tired faces and made a quick decision. He decided to tell a half-truth.

'No, no. You've done your best. Tomsk's a very strong swimmer, he'll turn up further down the Serpentine, or perhaps even in the Round Pond. I believe that there are some sort of underwater tunnels connecting the two ... Now then up with the pair of you. Good gracious me what is THAT!'

'I f-f-found it,' said Orinoco, whose teeth were starting to chatter. 'T-thought it was T-T-Tomsk at first. H-h-hit my head on it. C-c-could be dangerous to swimmers and b-b-boats so we brought it up with us. ATISHOOO.'

It turned out to be in an enormous metal object and it took a great deal of pushing and pulling before it was heaved out of the water and onto the shivering ice, which began to break up into little cracks and then much bigger ones.

'Quick,' commanded Great Uncle Bulgaria, quite forgetting his dignity for once and the five of them went slipping and sliding across the ice pushing the metal object ahead of them. It fairly skidded along, rather like an ungainly toboggan, and by the time they reached the bank they were travelling so fast that Bungo went head over heels with Wellington right behind him.

'Yow!' said Bungo.

'Wow!' shouted Wellington and he got to his back paws and made a dive for Great Uncle Bulgaria who was shaking the water out of his coat-sleeves.

'It's ... it's ... it's ... it's ...' gabbled Wellington.

'Tomsk?'

'No ...' Wellington gulped and pointed, his fur standing up in prickles, not from the cold but from fright. Everybody turned and looked and for a moment each Womble experienced the same prickly feeling as they looked at the large white thing which was coming towards them with its great white wings spread out.

With one accord Bungo, Wellington and Orinoco took refuge behind Tobermory, while Great Uncle Bulgaria said sternly:

'Behave yourselves, you silly young Wombles. It's only a swan!'

'It's ... it's ... it's IT,' gabbled Orinoco.

'Ho hum. That booklet if you please Wellington, the one on the waterways,' replied Great Uncle Bulgaria, whose mind was far more taken up with what had happened to Tomsk than the ridiculous way in which the three young Wombles were acting.

'Where can Tomsk have got to?' Great Uncle Bulgaria muttered to himself, 'silly great gormless Womble that he is ... AH HA! Yes, yes it says here "the overflow from the Serpentine normally discharges at the Eastern end into the

Ranelagh storm relief sewer (which crosses Hyde Park from the Bayswater Road to the Albert Gate) but if necessary valves . . ." '

'Bulgaria, old friend,' interrupted Tobermory, 'don't you think we should be sending out another search party rather than just standing here? Oh get away, you dratted bird!'

For the swan had now waddled round behind Tobermory and was pushing at him with its beak.

'I *am* working matters out,' Great Uncle Bulgaria said sternly. 'One moment please, Tobermory! . . . "if necessary, valves can be adjusted to carry the overflow to the lakes in Buckingham Palace Gardens and St James' Park." I w*onder* . . . Bungo, did you notice if there was any kind of current under water? Swan, stop that!'

For the swan was now prodding at Great Uncle Bulgaria's arm.

'Yes, there was rather,' said Bungo from behind the comforting form of Tobermory. 'I don't know why there should be a current when the Serpentine's only a lake, but . . .'

'*You* don't know anything! You think you do, but you don't. Swan – I said *stop* it! There is a possibility that Tomsk was carried along by that current, so that he may even now be surfacing in . . . Dear me, you are a most persistent bird!'

Great Uncle Bulgaria put the booklet into his damp coat pocket and looked through both pairs of spectacles at the swan and, in spite of his anxiety about Tomsk, a faint gleam of amusement came into his old eyes and he went on in quite a different tone of voice:

'Dear me, I wonder if you can be concerned with a "lace curtain", a devoted "watch dog" *and* a ghost?'

'Lot of nonsense,' grumbled Tobermory. He wasn't wearing boots and his back paws were distinctly chilly. Added to which he was very worried about Tomsk. He hauled the ladder on to the road and then, glancing at the big metal thing, added under his breath: 'Well I know what THAT is anyway, it's an old stove. Bulgaria, what about TOMSK!'

'Steady, steady,' replied Great Uncle Bulgaria who was now staring fixedly at the swan. He held out one white paw. 'Have you got a name, bird?'

'Hooooooo Hooooooo.'

'Yes, yes I see. Hoo-Hoo. No need to wake the whole Park though. You've dropped something, Hoo-Hoo. May I see what it is?'

Great Uncle Bulgaria leant over stiffly and picked up the scrap of rather damp paper which had fallen out of Hoo-Hoo's beak. He smoothed it out and looked at it carefully while everybody else, including Hoo-Hoo, watched him closely.

'You're Tomsk's friend, aren't you?' Great Uncle Bulgaria went on in the same quiet voice and, to everybody's astonishment, the swan lowered its long neck and nodded its head. 'So you'll help us find him, eh? Yes, yes, good bird. Good Hoo-Hoo. I want you to go and search for him. Look – for Tomsk. Find – Tomsk.'

Great Uncle Bulgaria spoke very slowly and distinctly, acting out his words as he spoke them. First pointing to Tomsk's abandoned snow-shoes and then sweeping one white paw in a semi-circle.

'FIND,' said Great Uncle Bulgaria, adding under his breath, 'animals have a great instinct for following the tracks of those they admire and it's worth a try. It's about the only hope we've got ... Tobermory!'

'Yes,' said Tobermory who had been goggling at this extraordinary behaviour, just as the others had been.

'Let the dog see the rabbit. Or, to be more precise, allow Hoo-Hoo to sniff Tomsk's snow-shoes. I'm sure that Hoo-Hoo has a very highly developed sense of smell ...'

Tobermory did as he was asked and Hoo-Hoo turned them

over with his beak. Then he turned to look at Great Uncle Bulgaria with sharp black eyes.

'Go – find.'

Hoo-Hoo hesitated for a second and then started to waddle onto the ice, he gained speed, his great wings spread out and he took to the air. He circled the gaping hole through which Tomsk had vanished, swooped down low over the Wombles and set off into a sky now turning pale with the approach of dawn.

'Well!' said Wellington.

'Well, well,' said Orinoco.

'Well, well, well,' said Bungo.

'What was in that note?' asked Tobermory.

Great Uncle Bulgaria smoothed out the wet crumpled paper on which a few words were carefully printed.

'Wubbleu under ice. Bird good. Bird find. Trust bird. Greetings. ow.'

'Ah HA,' said Tobermory slowly. 'But Bulgaria, old friend, it's a very slim chance . . .'

'It's the only one we've got,' said Great Uncle Bulgaria. 'If Tomsk had still been under the ice when Bungo and Orinoco went searching for him, they would have found him. Wombles can *always* search each other out. So he *must* have been swept out of the Serpentine. Now we must leave it to Hoo-Hoo . . . there's nothing else we *can* do. And, I may say, that once Tomsk returns – as I'm sure he will – I intend to search out this mysterious Mr ow and have a few words with him! Back to the burrow everybody!'

In spite of his optimistic words, Great Uncle Bulgaria felt more and more anxious as the next two hours dragged past with no further news of Tomsk. His cup of steaming acorn juice stood untouched by his side, and again and again he went to the door of the burrow to look up at the shining blue sky. There were many birds about, but there was no sign of the swan.

'Now look here, old friend,' said Tobermory, 'I'm going to throw this drink away because it's lukewarm and full of acorn grains, and I am going to get you another hot juice and then you are going to drink it AND explain one or two things.'

For once in his life Great Uncle Bulgaria allowed himself to be bossed about and meekly did as he was told.

'Well,' said Tobermory, sitting down opposite him and spreading his paws to the comforting glow of the electric fire, 'first of all, why lace-curtain-devoted-watchdog-part-of-the-ghost?'

'You know *Tomsk*,' said Great Uncle Bulgaria with a slight sigh, 'he's never the most talkative of Wombles. It took me a long while to get out of him just *how* he found that curtain, but it seems that the swan was choking on it, having got it stuck in its gullet, poor bird. I expect that ever since Tomsk freed it, the swan's been following him round trying to show its gratitude. Only Tomsk must have got it into his thick head that the bird was going to take a bite out of him. Tomsk's a very brave Womble, but . . .'

'Dear me,' said Tobermory with a faint smile, 'can't say I blame him. Swans can be vicious birds and they're powerful. I wouldn't care to have one treading on my heels every other minute. I have heard it said that they can break your arm with one swipe of their wings, but that may be just an old Wombles' tale. So that was why Tomsk was so jittery, but it still doesn't explain – or does it?'

Tobermory scratched behind his ear with his screwdriver, his smile grew wider and then he slapped one grey knee and chuckled. 'Don't tell me, let me guess! Tomsk got hold of the wrong end of the stick, as usual, and thought that when all the other silly young Wombles were whispering about the burrow being haunted they were talking about the swan and when . . .'

'Bungo asked him to describe it,' interrupted Great Uncle Bulgaria, wanting to finish the story himself. 'Tomsk said it was white with a long neck and on the large side. The swan, in fact, became our famous ghost! However, Tobermory, that still leaves us with the mystery of Mr ow. There were bootmarks in the snow right up to our front door and there's no doubt that it was he who pushed the door open to make us go and look for Tomsk.'

'Well if he got *that* far why didn't he come right inside?'

'I don't know, but I intend to find out. Now then,' Great Uncle Bulgaria was rapidly becoming his own brisk self, 'I want some money out of our money-trunk and a piece of writing paper and an envelope . . .'

'You're not writing to *The Times* again?'

'Yes I am. I am going to insert a message in the personal column addressed to ow, asking him to come forward, also to express our gratitude and to wish him a Happy Christmas.'

'Supposing he doesn't read *The Times*?'

'He will. Bound to. Next I want three pairs of boots and three white coats from the stores for Bungo, Orinoco and Wellington.'

'Wellington's got a coat on loan already.'

'So he has. Two then. When they are wearing them I want Orinoco to go to the post with my letter and Bungo and Wellington are to make their way to the Apsley Gate to watch for Tomsk.' Great Uncle Bulgaria paused, thinking deeply and then shook his head. 'It can't be helped,' he went on, 'I don't *like* sending my Wombles out in broad daylight, but it *is* a very cold morning and it is Sunday, so there won't be too many Human Beings about yet. However, I shall tell the three of them to be extremely cautious nevertheless. I do hope Tomsk remembers.'

'To be cautious?' asked Tobermory from the door.

'No, that old tunnel of ours which comes up in Constitution Hill. And while you're at it, old friend, I wouldn't mind another cup of acorn juice . . .'

'All right.' Tobermory peered into the cup Great Uncle Bulgaria was passing him. 'Tck, tck, tck. We really ought to strain this stuff more thoroughly. I'll have to think of some way of doing it . . .'

And Tobermory went off, tucking this small problem into the back of his mind to be dealt with at some future period when he had less to worry over.

Bungo, Orinoco and Wellington, who were all twice as nervous and anxious as Great Uncle Bulgaria and only half as good at hiding it – which made them all very twitchy indeed – were delighted to have something definite to do; although Orinoco did manage to nip back into the kitchen to pick up an orange-peel bun, just in case he should be overcome by the pangs of hunger while going to the letterbox.

'What *I* don't understand,' said Bungo as he and Wellington made their way across country to the Apsley Gate, 'is why old Tomsk should be coming back *this* way. I mean we don't even know where he's gone. Watch out, horses . . .'

They dived into the bushes until the early morning riders had cantered past, the horses skittering slightly for they'd got wind of the two young Wombles and Wombles and horses have never been very keen on each other.

'Then you weren't listening when Great Uncle Bulgaria read that piece out of the booklet. He thinks Tomsk's been carried down the overflow pipe from the Serpentine to the lake in the garden of Buckingham Palace.'

'Lumme, poor old Tomsk,' said Bungo with a shiver. 'But supposing Her lake is all frozen up too and Tomsk can't . . .' Bungo swallowed at the unpleasant idea which had just come into his mind.

'*She*'s got a lot of rare and valuable fish there as well as birds. So Her gardeners will make jolly sure that it's unfrozen.'

'Yes, but hang on.' Bungo's face was unusually furrowed at all this thinking he was having to do, 'I remember it said in that book thing that the water was pumped into St James' Park as well. Supposing Tomsk's gone there instead.'

'You could tell by the direction the swan took. I checked it on my compass. Any more questions?' said Wellington, very cheekily for him.

However, Bungo's rather battered pride was soon smoothed down, for Wellington very nearly walked straight on to the South Carriage Drive without looking out for traffic, and Bungo had to haul him back to safety as a large grey Rolls rather like 'WOM 1' purred past.

'Pooh, what a smell of petrol,' said Bungo. 'Yes, one more question, why did the Womble cross the road?'

At which Wellington biffed him one and Bungo biffed him back and they went happily on their way, peace restored, as there's nothing like a nice friendly little fight for making you feel better.

Their newly-found high spirits began to sag a bit though, as the hands on the clock on the side of the lodge by the Apsley Gate crept round and there was still no sign of their friend. Since they had to stay as hidden as possible there was little chance of moving about and, young though they were, they soon began to feel chilly as well as distinctly hungry. Snow clouds were piling up on the horizon and Bungo began to imagine himself and Wellington being turned into snow Wombles, when suddenly it got very dark indeed, right over their heads in fact. They both looked up and there, directly above them was a swan and at the same instant a chilling whisper said in their ears:

'It's large, it's white, it's woooooooo . . .'

'Yow!' said Bungo and Wellington and leapt into each other's arms.

'Hallo,' said Tomsk. His fur was covered with mud and earth, sticks and old dried leaves and he looked for all the world like a walking rubbish heap.

Bungo and Wellington rushed at him and hit him and pummelled him and slapped him on the back and shook his front paws violently, while Tomsk grinned from ear to ear and almost shook their arms out of their sockets.

'Sorry if I made you jump,' he said, 'I came up the subway and saw you sitting there and I couldn't help myself. Had quite a time of it, I have . . .'

Later in the burrow after a wash and brush down and an enormous meal (which earned him Orinoco's greatest respect), Tomsk was prompted to tell his story all over again. How he'd hit his head on something hard and sharp under the water and the next thing he knew was when he was being swept down the pipe, nearly getting stuck a couple of times as he got caught up with old bottles and things.

How all the underwater swimming he'd done had come in handy as it had taught him how to hold his breath for long periods. How he'd shot up out of the Buckingham Palace lake like a balloon and had then to duck down again because . . .'

'There was a boy out with his corgis?' piped up Wellington.

'That's right! He waved so I waved back, I hope that was all right?' Tomsk said with an anxious look at Great Uncle Bulgaria.

'Perfectly correct under the circumstances. Go on, Tomsk . . .'

How the swan had come circling down and driven off the other swans who'd come towards him hissing and stretching out their long necks. How, after thinking about it for some time he, Tomsk, had remembered that old tunnel that Wellington had dug last year and had sniffed it out and made use of it until he'd found himself in Constitution Hill.

'Had a bit of trouble then,' Tomsk said slowly.

'Trouble?' said Tobermory. 'What sort of trouble? Human Beings?'

'Not exactly. It was the swan. It would keep on walking *with* me instead of flying. It was very awkward. I didn't want to be rude to it . . .'

'Certainly not,' said Great Uncle Bulgaria, 'but I shouldn't let it worry you, Tomsk. THEY won't have noticed you under the circumstances, I'm sure . . .'

He was quite right as usual, for in Monday's *Times* there was a photograph of the swan waddling up Duke of Wellington Place, and underneath it were the words 'Royal Swan Takes A Walk'. In one corner of the picture it was just possible to make out a small fat figure wearing what appeared to be a very dirty fur coat.

Tomsk was now given two days off work, during which he nearly drove Tobermory distracted by saying over and over again:

'It was dreadfully, awfully, terribly mucky down there, you know. All kinds of rubbish and stuff. It can't be good for the fish or the birds, you know.'

'Yes, Tomsk. Just hold that vice for me, will you? Yes, Tomsk, but *we* can't stop Human Beings dumping their rubbish in the water.'

'Well somebody should tell them. It's all old plastic bags and bottles and dog-leads – supposing my swan swallowed one of those! – and boots and boxes. I'm glad Orinoco got that big metal stove out. And bits of wood and plates, cups, saucers and *millions* of lemonade bottles and tins. It can't be good for the fish, you know.'

'Yes, yes, yes I *do* know!'

'And old petrol cans and oil-cans. And some of them are leaking. That's the worst sort of Pollu and it can't be . . .'

'Tomsk,' said Tobermory very quietly. He leant against the workbench and ran his paw carefully over the sharp jagged edge of the metal wheel which was fixed in the vice. '*I* understand the problem, and you know and I know that water Pollu is one of the greatest enemies that we Wombles have to fight. But we have not yet discovered the *way* in which to fight it. Perhaps we never shall, in which case all the waterways, the rivers, the lakes, the seas and oceans of the world will become dreadfully, awfully, terribly mucky. But until somebody, somewhere works out the answer all we Wombles can do is to clear up some of the mess that Human Beings make.'

'Yes, but it can't be . . .'

'Never mind.' said Tobermory, who sometimes had the feeling that when he was talking to Tomsk he might just as well talk to the back of his own paw. 'Why don't you trot off and see if you can help Orinoco with that stove you've both been banging your heads against, eh?'

So Tomsk trotted, very glad to be out in the open air again. The snow had melted, so it was rather odd that a great white pile of what looked like snow was covering a lot of the bushes. Tomsk, a single-minded Womble, didn't stop to bother his head about this but went slipping and sliding to join his friends.

'Hallo Tomsk,' said Bungo, wiping one paw across his forehead, 'I say, do you think you can shift this thing?'

Tomsk dived into the bushes and put his sturdy arms round the stove, but although he pulled and struggled with all his might he only managed to move it a couple of inches.

'It's a whopper, isn't it?' said Orinoco patting the somewhat rusty monster proudly. 'I found it.'

'Yes, but I found it first,' said Tomsk. 'Morning, Hoo-Hoo.'

The swan arched its neck and settled into a sitting position with a flutter of its white feathers.

'We'll never get it back to the burrow,' said Orinoco. 'It's a problem, isn't it? I'll just settle back and have a little forty winks while I think over the matter.'

'I wish Wellington was here instead of stuck away in his silly old greenhouse,' said Bungo. 'He's quite good at *ideas*, although he's got hardly any stars on the chart, because he only brings in little bits of rubbish. The last star he got was for helping with that mangle . . .'

'With the hangle . . .' said Orinoco sleepily.

'Wellington's got a lot of quite good ideas really,' said Bungo generously. 'I suppose it's because he's almost a scientist. Scientists seem to have good ideas sometimes and sometimes,' Bungo went on, his voice growing faster, 'I have good ideas too! Look here Orinoco, if I manage to get this stove thing back to the burrow, can we go shares in it?'

Orinoco sat up quite briskly for him and there was no sleepiness at all in his bright little eyes as he looked from Bungo to the enormous stove and then up the long slippery slope which led to the burrow.

'I tell you what,' said Orinoco in an off-hand way, 'if you can get it back, then you can claim it as a find if I can have it *afterwards*.'

'That's jolly kind.'

'Yes, isn't it,' agreed Orinoco and settled back with his paws on his stomach.

A couple of minutes later a breathless Bungo fairly hurled himself into the Workshop and asked Tobermory for the use of two things.

'The mangle and some rope?' said Tobermory, looking up from a whole lot of bicycle chains which he was joining together. 'Very well, young Bungo, but what are you . . .'

But Bungo was already vanishing into the back store-room. It was a fascinating place with its rows and rows of shelves, each of which was stacked high with beautifully repaired and cleaned objects ranging from umbrellas to roller-skates, pram wheels to bicycle pedals, lemonade bottles to rugs, shopping baskets to gum-boots, iced-lolly sticks to ice-cream tubs, plastic spoons to transistor radios. While underneath the shelves were cupboards full of deck chairs, car seats, bicycle frames, roof racks, oars, vacuum cleaners, folding picnic tables, lawn mowers, and dozens of

other things. It always made Bungo think of Aladdin's Cave; but it was only the beginning of what the Wombles had managed to save and store, and would ultimately make use of. Beyond this was the wardrobe section with its gloves, scarves, hats, coats, boots, handkerchiefs, socks, briefcases and handbags. And then there was the linen department ... and the electrical department and the luggage department ... In fact they went on and on into the burrow and in each of them, hanging on the wall was a text embroidered by the Womblegarten which read

WASTE NOT WANT NOT!!!

Although sometimes the letters were a bit uneven.

However, at this particular moment Bungo was in too much of a tizzy to stop and admire everything, because he really had got rather a lot on his mind. What exactly this was became much clearer that evening, when Wellington nearly spoiled the whole business.

He was trotting across the Park with his white coat under his arm and that prickly feeling in his fur which told him that he was being watched by someone, somewhere, when he nearly tripped over a length of rope.

'Whoops,' said Wellington. 'What – who . . .'

'It's us. Me,' hissed Bungo, peering out of the gloom. 'And you nearly spoilt it. Come and lend a paw, old chap . . .'

And in no time flat the still bemused Wellington found himself beside Bungo turning the very heavy handle of the mangle. Wound round and round the rollers was one end of the rope and Wellington, somewhat breathlessly, did manage to inquire why a length of rope needed mangling.

'Just keep turning,' said Bungo, 'explain later . . . hallo here she comes . . .'

And out of the winter gloaming there appeared very slowly, and with a lot of squelching noises, the enormous stove, with Tomsk and Orinoco shoving at it from behind.

Like some great whale it wallowed into the burrow, nearly getting stuck in the corridor until it finally came to rest just short of the Workshop.

'My word,' said Tobermory, scratching away at his ear harder than ever.

'Tck, tck, tck, tck,' said Great Uncle Bulgaria. 'Words nearly fail me, Bungo! You've certainly done extremely well to – er – rescue this bit of old iron. It must have come out of some hotel . . .'

'It's not bad is it?' agreed Bungo, who in spite of being very out of breath was seeing his Gold Medal more clearly than ever before. In fact it almost seemed to be dancing up and down before his eyes. Bungo blinked and rubbed and saw that he was actually looking at one of Madame Cholet's ladles which she had clutched in one paw.

'Regard,' said Madame Cholet, now waving the ladle at the stove.

'We *are* regarding,' said Great Uncle Bulgaria. 'And it's quite remarkable.'

'I found it,' said Orinoco.

'I found it first,' said Tomsk.

'But I got it back to the burrow,' said Bungo. 'At least it was my idea about *how* to get it back, wasn't it Tobermory?'

'Ho hum. Yes, yes Bungo it was.'

'Of course everybody helped,' said Bungo, 'and thank you all very much, but now that it is here it will be worth a lot of stars on the chart, won't it?'

'Ye-es,' said Tobermory, stroking his chin.

'And after *that*,' said Orinoco from the back of the group, 'after *that*, don't forget you said I could claim it.'

Six Womble heads turned slowly in his direction and Orinoco shuffled his back paws and tried not very successfully to look both innocent and modest.

'You see,' he said, 'I think this lovely stove is going to be my particular way of fighting Pollu. And Bungo, old friend, I'm ever so grateful to you for getting it back here . . .'

Great Uncle Bulgaria, Tobermory and Madame Cholet exchanged glances and all three of them hastily put their paws up to their mouths. Great Uncle Bulgaria was the first to recover his composure. He leant towards Tobermory and said in a somewhat unsteady whisper:

'Snookered, is, I think the correct expression, don't you old friend . . .?'

'Or mandled perhaps?' said Tobermory.

Wellington was only very dimly aware that the friendship between Orinoco and Bungo had become rather strained, because he'd got a lot of other things on his mind. Tomsk didn't even realize that anything was wrong at all, as he had his own particular problem – or rather problems to deal with – the strange pieces of white stuff which he kept picking up by the armful from all round the edges of, and sometimes floating in, the Serpentine. Some of the sillier birds would keep thinking it was bread or sandwiches but, when they tried to eat it, it stuck in their beaks and they would go swimming round and round in circles choking and spluttering, till Tomsk managed to catch them and shake it out of them.

Tomsk appealed to Tobermory for extra help, but after the short, sharp cold spell, Spring had come early and with it crowds of Human Beings who seemed to be dropping more litter than ever. So every working Womble was at full stretch and Tobermory had no one he could spare.

'It's no good asking *me*,' said Orinoco, who besides being on normal tidying up duty was also working on what he rather grandly referred to as his 'stove project'. 'Why not ask you-know-who?'

'If,' said Bungo with chilly dignity. '*If*, a certain Womble is suggesting *me* – and my name by the way happens to be Bungo – then I am afraid I cannot assist you. *I* have a "heavy load project" which is taking up all *my* time.'

Tomsk thought this over for some while and came to the conclusion that it all added up to meaning 'no go'.

'O.K.,' he said and lumbered off, pausing by the door. 'But I do know your name Bungo. I've known it ever since you've had it actually. Well I'll just have to try Wellington that's all . . .'

Tomsk got quite a shock when he ran Wellington to earth in his little greenhouse.

'You've been overdoing it,' he said, 'your fur's turned white!'

'Has it?'

Wellington hit himself briskly and clouds of dust rose in all directions. When this cleared it became obvious that Wellington's fur, although still rather grey, was its normal colour beneath this coating.

'What are you doing?' asked Tomsk.

'Inventing.'

'Inventing what?'

'Well, I shan't know till I've invented it, shall I?'

'No, I suppose not.'

Wellington went back to stirring a pinky-brown liquid in what had once been a lemonade bottle. There was a whole row of these bottles on a shelf, all of them full of different coloured liquids and neatly labelled; while in one corner a scrubbed-out petrol drum contained something which looked like white mud. It was moving slightly and was making a funny 'squelch-squelch' sound, and every few seconds a fat bubble would rise to the surface and then grow larger and larger until it burst with a faint 'plop'. Next to this, was a step-ladder which Wellington had neatly converted into a row of little shelves, on which reposed a line of seed-boxes with small green seedlings already showing through the earth. There was also a collection of flower-pots with geranium cuttings in them and a great stack of books, leaflets, coloured charts and diagrams; while some strange-shaped glasses, bottles and tubes were arranged in what had once been a plastic sink tidy.

'I *say*,' said Tomsk, deeply impressed.

He sniffed, his head on one side. There was a faint, sweet scent of flowers in the air, which was very pleasant and which stirred in him distant memories of long hot summer days.

'It's nice,' said Tomsk, 'next to the smell of Madame Cholet's leaf puddings, it's the nicest smell I've ever smelt.'

'Thank you,' said Wellington absentmindedly. 'I quite like it myself. Move over, there's a good Womble . . .'

What with the pair of them, and all the rest of the stuff that Wellington had accumulated, the little greenhouse was

somewhat overcrowded and Tomsk only just stopped himself from sitting backwards into the bubbling white mud.

Wellington went 'tck, tck, tck' under his breath, but was too polite to say anything more. Then, to Tomsk's alarm, his friend produced a small piece of plastic garden hose out of his pocket and put one end in his mouth and the other into the pink-brown liquid and sucked.

'Here, steady . . .' whispered Tomsk. 'If you don't know what that stuff is it might be poison, you know . . .'

But Wellington only waved him away with one paw; and then he did something even more amazing, for with one swift movement he took the tube out of his mouth, put his paw over the top of it and then he removed the other end of the tube from the pinky-brown stuff – but not a drop fell out of the tube.

Tomsk's eyes bulged. It was like magic, and his fur got a creepy feeling.

Wellington didn't appear to be surprised in the least. In fact, with a corner of his pink tongue showing at the side of his mouth because he was concentrating so hard, he picked up an old kitchen strainer and held it over some of the seedlings; and then very gently shifted his paw a little on the top of the tube and a few drops of the pinky-brown liquid splattered out and fell into the strainer and then on to the seedlings.

'Steady, good, fine . . .' muttered Wellington, and then dropped the now empty tube and the strainer into a fire bucket full of water, wiped his paws down the front of his jacket and, looking up at the bulging-eyed Tomsk, said calmly:

'Yes, what was it you wanted? Is it dinner-time?'

Tomsk shook his head dumbly.

'You all right?' inquired Wellington.

'Yes. But . . . but, Wellington why didn't that stuff come out of the tube?'

'Suction. You can do the next batch of seedlings if you like.'

'No thank you,' said Tomsk hastily. 'I say, Wellington, are all the things in here yours?'

'Um hum. I collected them and cleaned them and Tobermory gave me permission to use them.'

'But supposing they catch you doing it.'

'They won't. They only work here in the daytime and when I'm not here I lock the door and put this on it.'

And Wellington brought out from under his bench a large square of cardboard on which was written:

PRIVATE

Please Keep Out Unless
On Official Business.

Signed. W.W.

'I leave the key hanging beside it, so they can come in if they want to. After all, it is their greenhouse,' said Wellington fairmindedly. 'And I tie a piece of black thread just across the lock. But I've never found it broken yet. Human Beings aren't very inquisitive, you know. I'll never understand them if I live to be two hundred. Well?'

'Well what?'

'Well, what do you want me for? If you don't mind me mentioning it I *am* a bit busy. I want to try some Dis M on my Step 4s.'

'*Do* you?' said Tomsk, now absolutely befogged.

'It's quite simple. I'll explain if you like. Those lemonade bottles are all labelled from A to P. P's as far as I've got up till now. So the first bottle is Discovery A, or Dis A for short. Then Step 4 is the fourth step up from the ground on my ladder-shelves. Now the cuttings over there I'm treating in quite a different way. I've labelled them AA, BB, CC and so on, while the cuttings in the flower-pots are – I say, are you going Tomsk?'

'Hm, hm,' said Tomsk, nodding and retreating backwards. He had an uneasy feeling that at any moment Wellington might slap a label on *him* and turn him into T/W or some such thing.

'Pity, I was rather enjoying explaining to *someone*. Shhh – what's that?'

Wellington half rose to his back paws, his fur going stiff. Tomsk turned round and, glancing over his shoulder, said:

'Only old Hoo-Hoo. Follows me everywhere, you know. What did you think it was?'

'Oh nothing. Only, although we know now that the burrow's not haunted, I still get this feeling I'm being watched. It's not very nice.'

'There's nobody here now but us three. You've been over-doing it I expect. Too much thinking, that's your trouble.'

Wellington nodded doubtfully and then looked at the swan which was preening itself.

'I tell you what,' Wellington said suddenly, 'I suppose you couldn't sort of *lend* Hoo-Hoo to me? I'd feel quite safe if he was here. That is if you wouldn't *mind*, Tomsk?'

'Mind? I'd be jolly glad. I don't want to hurt his feelings but he does get in the way a bit. I'll tell him what he's got to do . . .'

It took quite a lot of telling, but Tomsk was a very patient Womble and, although the swan drooped sulkily when for about the fiftieth time Tomsk turned him to the right-about and returned him to Wellington, he finally crouched down by the greenhouse door and stayed there.

'That's a good bird,' said Tomsk, feeding him a piece of bread. 'See you later then.'

'Thanks awfully,' said Wellington, 'but look here, you never did tell me what you wanted . . .'

'Doesn't matter,' replied Tomsk and went off whistling under his breath. It really was a relief *not* to have Hoo-Hoo treading on his heels for a bit.

So Wellington returned happily to his discoveries and because he was working so hard he got even more absent-minded than ever, and once or twice, after he'd locked up for the day, he might have set off in entirely the wrong direction if Hoo-Hoo hadn't nipped hold of his coat and set him to the right-about. He still got the creepy feeling from time to time but the swan seemed to get it too and would go scutling off hissing and flapping his great wings, until whatever-it-was went away.

'I suppose you know you've only got two stars on the chart,' said Bungo.

'Yes,' said Wellington vaguely. 'I wonder if I crossed Dis C with Dis R whether it might work. What do you think?'

'I think you've gone a bit . . .' and Bungo tapped the side of his head with one paw.

'Probably,' agreed Wellington and drifted away with his paws sunk into the pockets of his white coat, leaving Bungo staring after him. Bungo was feeling a bit lonely these days, what with Orinoco forever tapping and tinkering away at his stove and Tomsk spending all his time down at the Serpentine or the Round Pond. And as for old Wellington, he sometimes forgot to come into meals and, for a Womble, that was quite extraordinary.

Bungo went off slowly to have another look at the star chart to reassure himself that all was still well with the world; and then, passing the great mound of white stuff which now had a part of the burrow all to itself and a notice saying, 'Compressed Plastic Foam (Polystyrene) Please dump here. Signed. Tobermory W.', he suddenly made up his mind and went to see Great Uncle Bulgaria.

The old Womble listened to Bungo in silence and then said gruffly:

'All work and no play makes a dull Womble, eh? Never mind, young Bungo, we'll have a big party in the summer when I make my little speech and present the Gold Medal, so you've got *that* to look forward to. But you're quite right to tell me about Wellington and perhaps he *is* overdoing it. Leave it to me . . .'

It was a fine Spring dawn when Great Uncle Bulgaria set off to pay a call on Wellington. The old Womble sniffed the air with pleasure as he walked briskly across the grass, although he wrinkled his white nose in disgust as he crossed the Serpentine Road, for, with his still keen sense of smell, he was aware of a lingering whiff of exhaust fumes here. In all directions he could see silent bands of Wombles at work. Through the trees he caught a glimpse of Miss Adelaide with a line of very small Wombles trotting along behind her. She was teaching them the lay-out of the Park and showing them the best places to hide, should any Human Being suddenly appear. Tomsk was down by the Serpentine shovelling litter into his extra large tidy-bag, watched by an admiring ring of black-backed gulls, herring gulls, a kestrel, a great many mallards and even the lordly heron which was standing thoughtfully on one leg. Orinoco, who'd been having a nice forty winks, cosily tucked up in the hollow trunk of an old elm tree, hastily heaved himself out and began picking up crumpled newspapers and Bungo was trying to push an ancient garden roller up a slight slope.

Great Uncle Bulgaria paused, opened his mouth to call out and then closed it again. Young Bungo thought he knew the answer to everything, so it would do him no harm to learn a little lesson the hard way. Great Uncle Bulgaria leant on his stick and waited patiently and sure enough, Bungo, having reached the top of the small hill and obviously very pleased with himself, paused for a breather. He then discovered that what goes up, quite often goes down, and suddenly the roller began to trundle on its way, gathering speed as it did so.

A faint cry of 'Oi – stop – oi' was wafted across the Park and the last view Great Uncle Bulgaria had of Bungo was of that young Womble hanging on desperately to the long handle of the roller, before he and it had both vanished over the brow of the bank.

Great Uncle Bulgaria proceeded calmly on his way until he reached the greenhouse where he knocked politely. Hoo-Hoo regarded him suspiciously and then sank back and went on preening his beautiful wings. Great Uncle Bulgaria knocked again and then again and again, at which a muffled voice said:

'Come in. Door's not locked.'

Things had changed quite a bit since Tomsk had called in on Wellington. The lemonade bottles had been reduced to two, Dis A/3 and Dis Y/2, and the white mud had stopped bubbling. All the seedlings and cuttings had grown enormously and the sweet, summery smell was very strong indeed and seemed to have attracted a large number of early bees. Some of them were climbing sleepily along the shelves while others crept with most un-bee-like slowness along the work bench.

Great Uncle Bulgaria took all this in at a glance but, what really caught his attention and made a shiver of horror run through his white fur, was Wellington. For Wellington had his face buried in his front paws and his shoulders were shaking.

'My dear, dear Womble,' said Great Uncle Bulgaria, gently but firmly clasping Wellington's arm, 'what is it? are you ill? Has something dreadful happened?'

'Yes,' said Wellington in a husky whisper. 'I'm finished, done, defeated. My experiments have all gone wrong.'

'Suppose you stop feeling quite so sorry for yourself, blow your nose and try and explain calmly and clearly, instead of like a silly cry-Womble. I thought you were a *scientist*!'

At these harsh words Wellington sat up, wiped his misted spectacles and blew his nose on the end of his scarf. He drew a deep breath, frowned and thrust his front paws into his pockets.

'Sorry,' he said gruffly and then cleared his throat and went on in a more normal voice. 'I really thought I was making a great discovery. I was discovering two things. First how to make plants extra strong so that they wouldn't catch germs or be attacked by pests: and secondly how to make them smell even nicer to the bees.'

'You certainly succeeded there,' said Great Uncle Bulgaria. 'I haven't seen so many bees in years.'

Wellington heaved up an enormous sigh which shook him from head to toe.

'Oh yes,' he agreed mournfully. 'But I've made it *too* strong. It sends them all off to sleep, and it takes them ages to wake up again because my SS3 . . .'

' "SS3" – what's that?'

'Sweet Scent, third attempt. Scientists always give their discoveries numbers instead of names. It's shorter and ... and ...'

'More scientific altogether. I see. And?'

'It's sort of sticky. Well, very sticky actually, so it sticks to the bees. While as for my Dis A/3 and Dis Y/2 – well Great Uncle Bulgaria, just look!'

Great Uncle Bulgaria turned his full attention to the pots of geraniums ... swallowed ... adjusted both his pairs of spectacles ... put his face close up to the flowers and then turned very slowly and stared at Wellington.

'Yes,' said Wellington, more miserably than ever. 'It's true all right. I've grown the first *blue* geraniums in the world. And green alyssum and orange lobelia and yellow salvias and purple daisies and white dandelions and I've got some pinky-white buttercups if you'd care to look ...'

'No thank you,' said Great Uncle Bulgaria. 'Oh, my dear, *dear* Wellington! But tell me just one thing more. What do you think would happen if you mixed Dis A/3 and Dis Y/2?'

'I don't know. Oh I daren't, Great Uncle Bulgaria. I just daren't!'

'And you call yourself a scientist! What's in those two bottles anyway?'

'Lots and lots and lots of things. Stewed elm bark, conifer needles, dried chestnut leaves, moss, mud from the Round Pond, peat, holly berries, sycamore . . .'

'Stop, stop that's enough. Nothing *harmful* then?'

'Well no, not in a way. I mean it's all grown naturally. That was the whole point, you see. I was discovering something *good* to help the plants. Something without any *chemicals* in it. I was fighting plant Pollu.'

'Then go ahead and mix 'em. It's no good stopping now. You may be on the brink of something really important. Use that bucket.'

With somewhat trembling paws Wellington reluctantly did as he was told. He had scrubbed out that particular bucket, but he hadn't used it before and some instinct now made him place it carefully outside the greenhouse. Then, trembling still more, he poured in all the contents of the first bottle and then those of the second bottle. Nothing happened at all, apart from a few rainbow-coloured bubbles rising to the surface.

'Oh well,' said Wellington, feeling both disappointed and relieved at this tame finish. 'That's that then. Mind out, Great Uncle Bulgaria, there's some oil behind you on the ground, and you might pick up diesel paw like poor old Orinoco did.'

'What will you do now?' asked Great Uncle Bulgaria following Wellington back into the greenhouse.

'Clear away my books and notes,' said Wellington with a bleak smile, 'clean everything up and leave it as I found it. And compost those plants. It's a shame really, because they're quite pretty in a way . . .'

Wellington set to work and Great Uncle Bulgaria, who

knew that there's nothing like keeping busy for taking your mind off your troubles, let him get on with it. He felt very, very sorry for Wellington, who had laboured so hard and so long, and then been defeated, but he also knew that to say this aloud might only make the young Womble full of self-pity, so he held his tongue.

It was Hoo-Hoo who broke up this somewhat melancholy scene. He suddenly hissed and then hooted and then there was a scrabbling sound and a beating of wings and the large bird rose up into the air, flying round and round in circles.

'Dratted thing,' mumbled Great Uncle Bulgaria and turned round to see what all the trouble was about. But there was nobody there and no scent of a Human Being and he was just going to stump back into the greenhouse when he had an odd feeling that there was something missing somewhere. He peered to left and right, but the rows and rows of giant greenhouses were quite as usual, their great glass roofs and walls glittering in the increasing sunlight.

There was the big wheelbarrow he'd noticed earlier and the piles of flower pots and broken glass and . . .

'Lumme!' said Great Uncle Bulgaria. It was not a word he normally used, but it was surprised out of him. He wiped a corner of his tartan shawl across his forehead and then said in a very gruff voice.

'Wellington, come here.'

'Yes. Great Uncle Bulgaria,' said Wellington dolefully.

'And look there . . .'

The old Womble pointed with his stick at the ground before them. It was a perfectly ordinary piece of ground, apart from a small puddle which even now was drying out in the warm sunshine. Wellington looked at it dutifully, frowned and then looked up at Great Uncle Bulgaria, who said slowly:

'And *where* is that plastic bucket, pray? Not to mention the oil?'

'Gone!' said Wellington. 'Vanished! *Dissolved!*'

'So it would seem. No wonder he took to the air. It must have given him quite a turn, poor bird.'

'But how can we be sure that it was MY mixture that's made everything vanish?' asked Wellington in a whisper.

'Look at the ground round about young Womble. Nothing has walked on it or touched it in any way. There's not a foot-mark or a paw-mark to be seen. Nothing and nobody has come near your bucket – I beg your pardon, your ex-bucket. Even Hoo-Hoo obviously kept well clear of it. Instinct I suppose, he must have realized that something unusual was taking place. Quite intelligent birds, swans. One day I intend to write a letter to *The Times* about them. You were saying?'

'Dis A/3 and Dis Y/2 mixed in equal quantities,' mumbled Wellington. 'They CAN'T have . . . but they HAVE LUMMEE!'

'What a very vulgar expression, young Womble. Please

try *not* to use it,' said Great Uncle Bulgaria at his most serene. 'I trust, Wellington that you have your notes safely?'

But Wellington, in a most un-Womble like way, was beyond speech.

For some time after this Wellington appeared to be going round in a daze, and Bungo, who in spite of his bossiness had a very kind heart, decided to take matters into his own paws. It seemed to him that, for once, Great Uncle Bulgaria just hadn't been able to cope with Wellington's problem, so when Bungo saw a notice which said, 'Great Pop Festival Week. Bring Your Friends.' it occurred to him that this was exactly the sort of jaunt that Wellington needed.

'It'll do you good,' Bungo said earnestly. 'All work and no play makes Wellington a dull Womble, you know, and I feel pretty dull myself actually.'

'Um,' said Wellington. 'It dissolved. Vanished. *All* of it!'

'That's right,' agreed Bungo, 'so it did. All gone . . .' and he waved his paws.

'All, all gone,' Wellington nodded.

'Tck, tck, tck you *are* in a bad way. Now listen, Wellington? Wellington?' Bungo snapped his claws in front of his friend's bemused face. 'We're going to a Festival. You'd like that wouldn't you? Oh dear! Oh lor! Oh me! Wellington . . .'

'Yes?'

'Never mind. Just come along with me, your old friend Bungo. I'll look after you. Only I don't think we'd better tell anybody else. Great Uncle Bulgaria's not all that keen on us mixing with Human Beings. I wish Orinoco'd come as well, but he's forever tinkering about with that old stove. I don't think he'll get it to work and I don't believe Madame Cholet does either; and as for Tomsk, he's always splashing about so *he* won't come . . .'

It was on a lovely cool and apparently calm Spring evening that Bungo dragged Wellington out of the burrow and alternately pushed and pulled him down towards the Serpentine. As they came over a ridge in the ground Bungo halted, his ears going back. Having read the notice very carefully he knew that the Concert had been going on since the middle of the morning. But as the Wombles work at dusk and into the night (they can see quite well in the dark) and again at dawn they are, naturally enough, cosily asleep for a lot of the day. And as the Hyde Park burrow is extremely well built and very deep it is also nice and quiet, so the noises and sounds of the outside world don't reach it. But now those noises reached both Bungo and Wellington all too clearly.

'Is that – is that *music*?' asked Wellington, coming out of his dazed state.

'It's a *sort* of music,' said Bungo.

'It's not like the sort of music that Great Uncle Bulgaria made us listen to in the Autumn.'

(Great Uncle Bulgaria had taken a small and carefully chosen party of Wombles to hear the last night of the Proms from the Albert Hall*. He had made them all sit on the steps that led up to the Albert Memorial and had, himself, conducted them in singing *Rule Britannia*. It had been a very stirring occasion, during which Miss Adelaide had been seen to be actually *sniffing*.)

'It's just *different*, that's all,' Bungo replied firmly, 'and you're going to enjoy it.'

'*Am* I?'

'Yes!'

Wellington somehow doubted it, but he knew that Bungo

* The Promenade Concerts.

was trying to be kind so he dutifully followed his friend down the bank, through the bushes and so to the edge of the Serpentine where both of them paused in astonishment. The roar that was coming over the amplifiers was now quite deafening and, as they weren't used to very loud sounds, the ears of the two young Wombles began to ache a bit. But that wasn't all, for ahead of them and closely packed together were hundreds and hundreds and HUNDREDS of young Human Beings swaying backwards and forwards to the beat of the music. Human Beings eating sandwiches and drinking fizzy lemonade. Human Beings who looked as if they were fast asleep in spite of the dreadful din. Human Beings jumping up and down and Human Beings singing – at least their mouths were opening and shutting.

'I didn't know there were so many of them,' whispered Wellington.

'What?' bellowed Bungo.

Wellington gulped and spread his front paws wide and then swept them round in a half-circle.

Bungo nodded violently, as though he understood what this meant, and then pushed the reluctant Wellington further down the bank until they were on the edge of the crowd. There was obviously no need to be worried that they might be noticed as being Wombles, for all the Human Beings round them were wearing all kinds of strange clothes from long nightgown sort of things to fur coats.

The two Wombles sat down, their little eyes as round as buttons as they looked about them. Never had they seen anything like this before and, although they didn't understand it, it was all very interesting.

'Perhaps', thought Bungo, 'they *like* all being squashed together. I suppose it's all right if they've got nice large burrows to go home to. But I wouldn't care for it if all us Wombles were right on top of each other. I mean I *like* other Wombles and I've got a lot of *friends*, but it's nice to

be on your own sometimes, so that you can just stop and look at and listen to and sniff at things . . .'

'Perhaps,' thought Wellington, completely forgetting his vanishing plastic bucket and the diesel oil for the first time in several days, 'perhaps they *like* lots of noise . . .' His head was starting to buzz with the continual 'thump-thump' of the music vibrating in his ears.

Suddenly the bewildered Wellington became aware that someone seemed to be squeezing his way through the crowd towards him. Next, a short, square sort of person, wearing a white towelling robe complete with hood, sat down beside him.

'Greeting, Wubleuu,' growled a deep voice.

Wellington was too bemused to be astonished or even afraid and he just stared, goggled-eyed at the stranger.

'Da, da,' rumbled the voice, 'I have a message for you to take to Great Little Uncle Bulgaria.'

'What?' yelled Wellington, who, what with the noise and the overcrowded surroundings, was starting to feel distinctly unwell.

'Message,' roared the voice.

Several Human Beings and Bungo turned in Wellington's direction and made the sort of faces which mean 'Shh – shut up!'

Wellington blinked and decided that enough was enough. All right, if Bungo liked this sort of party then that was *his* affair, but as for him, Wellington, he wanted no more part of it. So Wellington gripped his front paws into fists, stuffed them firmly over his ears, wriggled his way out of the crowd and began to walk fast and then faster and faster away from the party on the Serpentine until his small back paws were going very rapidly indeed and he was running as quickly as he could.

Crash! Biff! Wallop!

Wellington collided with something extremely solid and reeled backwards. For one frightening moment he thought he'd gone full tilt into one of the policemen who patrolled the Park during the evening and at night, and then a voice said reassuringly:

'Hallo, young Womble, what's all the hurry?'

'Sorry,' said Wellington. 'Oh it's you, Tobermory, you and the Silver Womble!'

'Tck, tck, tck, you *are* in a state, just calm down, young Womble, and listen to the nightingales ... You've got a touch of Noise-Pollu by the look of you ...'

They leant against the solid shape of the Wombles' own car and after a while Wellington said shyly:

'I like it when it's sort of quiet, don't you? I mean we can hear the music from here and the traffic, but it's not all on top of us. Do you like the Park, Tobermory?'

'Yes. There's six hundred acres of it, young Womble. They call the Royal Parks the lungs of London. If it wasn't for this

grass and those trees and the bushes and all the rest of it, that part of London'd be all streets and houses and that's a terrible thought. Great Uncle Bulgaria tells me that you've made a Great Discovery.'

'Well, p'raps,' Wellington wriggled his back paws in the grass, 'sort of. Maybe. Don't know yet, really.'

'Ho hum. And where's young Bungo?'

'He's – um – he's . . .' said Wellington and waved one paw vaguely in the direction of the Serpentine. A piece of paper, which he hadn't realized until then he'd been clutching, drifted away in the soft Spring breeze and Wellington dived after it automatically and smoothed it out.

'Bus ticket?' said Tobermory, who had turned back to the Silver Womble and was tinkering with the engine.

'Yes – no – oh! It's a letter and it's addressed to Great *Little* Uncle Bulgaria. Somebody must have pushed it into my paw down by – at the – just now when – that is – oh dear!'

'Tck, tck, тск,' said Tobermory, 'well you'd better deliver it, hadn't you? And don't worry about Bungo, I'm keeping an eye on him.'

'Oh . . .' gulped Wellington and headed back for the burrow, wondering as he ran just how the older Wombles always seemed to know what was going on . . .

Great (Little) Uncle Bulgaria appeared to accept the letter just as calmly as Tobermory had done, although once he had sent Wellington off to the kitchen to have a nice calming mug of hot chocolate and dandelion juice, he did sit up a great deal more sharply as he murmured:

'Funny way to go about things, but then I suppose it's only to be expected. Well, let's see what Mr O W has to say this time. Ah HA. "Am trustering you". Dear me what odd spelling. "Am trustering you to meet with me on neutral soil. Is by Speakerers' Corner," Tck, tck, tck, "at sunset. Regards. O W".'

Great Uncle Bulgaria shook his head and then looked up as Tobermory appeared in the doorway.

'Sit down, old friend,' said Great Uncle Bulgaria. 'I have something to tell you about our mysterious friend Mr O W; but before I go into that, have you anything to report?'

'Not much,' grunted Tobermory. 'Bungo's still at that dratted Pop Affair, jumping up and down and pretending he's enjoying it. He'll be stone deaf for a couple of days after this I shouldn't wonder. Orinoco's got his stove into position at last and is having a nice forty winks to recover his strength. Wellington's come out of the clouds and will be as right as rain by dawn. Madame Cholet and Miss Adelaide are friends again and Tomsk is *still* mumbling on about the birds and the fish. What else would you like to know?'

'Ah HA,' Great Uncle Bulgaria looked over his spectacles. 'I suppose it's no good inquiring what *you've* been up to?'

'No good at all,' said Tobermory, 'heh, heh, heh. Well?'

'Well Mr O W has decided to come out into the open at last. If ever I met such a mysterious creature! The rendezvous he has chosen is Speakers' Corner at sunset. Will you come with me?'

'Try and keep me away,' replied Tobermory and rubbed behind his silky grey ear even more vigorously than usual.

The somewhat reduced thump-thump-thump of the Pop Concert was still vibrating across the Park as Great Uncle Bulgaria and Tobermory started to walk towards Speakers' Corner. They kept well to the north of the Serpentine, crossing Buck Hill Walk and then the West Carriage Drive and so, following an old Womble track which was both peaceful and beautiful, they approached Speakers' Corner.

'Free Speech,' murmured Great Uncle Bulgaria, hitching up his tartan shawl, 'it's one of the few freedoms left in this overcrowded world of ours. Why I can remember . . .'

'Yes, yes, yes,' said Tobermory, who knew from experience when Great Uncle Bulgaria was about to make one of his own little speeches, 'dear me, what a lot of rubbish they do leave about to be sure. We'll have to send an extra working party out tomorrow, that's certain. And *just* when we're particularly short-pawed. Who is that Human Being with the large crowd listening to him?'

'That's Lord Soper,' said Great Uncle Bulgaria. 'And a very fine speaker he is, too. He comes here regularly. While on that platform there . . .'

Great Uncle Bulgaria described the scene in detail. As he very much enjoyed making speeches himself he fully appreciated other professionals in the same line of business and, more than once, he had been tempted to climb up on to a wooden crate and to say a few words on his own particular subject of fighting Pollu.

'Now what do we do?' mumbled Tobermory.

'We wait for Mr OW.'

So they waited and waited and waited, while the sky above turned from violet to purple and then to dark blue and, as Wombles – at least old Wombles – are very patient creatures, it was no particular hardship. And anyway there were plenty of things to watch, with all the traffic whirling endlessly round Marble Arch and then down the Bayswater Road, or up Oxford Street or down Park Lane. And apart from the cars, the vans, the lorries, the buses, the motorcycles, the taxis and the mopeds, there were crowds and crowds of Human Beings wandering about on foot.

'Haven't they got any burrows to go to?' murmured Tobermory. 'I'll never understand Human Beings, not if I live to be *three* hundred!'

'Greetings,' said a deep voice.

'Evening,' replied Tobermory.

'Password?' inquired the voice out of the gloom.

'OW,' said Great Uncle Bulgaria briskly, 'and as you know very well who I am and who Tobermory is and why we're all here, please don't let's waste any more time on any more of this ridiculous cloak-and-dagger stuff. We will now, all three of us, walk slowly away from here and back to the burrow.'

'Da,' growled the voice.

'If you mean "yes", then kindly say so,' said Great Uncle Bulgaria sharply. 'I'm quite certain that your English is as good as, if not better than, my Russian.'

On either side of the old Womble there was a distinct feeling of surprise from his two companions, but Great Uncle Bulgaria continued to walk in a westerly direction, his stick thudding on the grass, his wise little black eyes looking neither to left nor right.

'Look here, Bulgaria,' said Tobermory. 'what *is* all this?'

'I don't know about *all*,' replied Great Uncle Bulgaria, without pausing in his measured progress down the ancient Womble path which led across the Park. 'All I am certain of is that a certain Other Womble has been hanging round our burrow and spying on us for several months. Why that Other Womble should behave in this manner is his own affair, but I for one have had more than enough of it. Should that Other Womble care to speak up I am perfectly prepared to listen, as I know you are, Tobermory.'

Tobermory blinked, got the message and wisely kept quiet.

The progress of the three Wombles continued slowly across the Park, with Great Uncle Bulgaria very slightly in the lead, while two larger and more bulky figures trailed behind him. Nobody spoke a word, even when they reached the doorway of the burrow, and if Tomsk's eyes became as round as penny pieces as he marked them down in the Duty Book, that was his affair.

Great Uncle Bulgaria stumped into his study, nodded to Tobermory to close the door and then sank down into his rocking-chair, while he waved the third member of the party to the seat opposite him.

'Well, young Womble?' said Great Uncle Bulgaria, and he looked over the top of his spectacles in that particular way which had made many a Womble tremble in his (or her) fur. 'What have you got to say for yourself?'

There was quite a long pause and then the strange Womble stepped forward and stood stiffly to attention, clicking his back paws together as he did so. He was about the same size and probably about the same age as Tomsk.

'My number is . . .'

'Number, number, number,' interrupted Great Uncle Bulgaria, 'I don't want any *number*, you great gormless Womble, I want your name. Come on, and stop shuffling about . . .'

'Is Omsk,' said the strange Womble in a deep rumbling voice. 'Name is Omsk.'

'Get on,' said Tobermory from the shadows. 'It never *is*! Omsk! So much for your "Other Womble", Bulgaria old friend! Heh, heh, heh. Omsk!'

'Is nothing fonny,' said Omsk. 'Is very *good* name.'

'Omsk,' said Tobermory doubling up and hitting his knees with his paws. 'Omsk . . . ooooo.'

'Omsk,' said Great Uncle Bulgaria beginning to chuckle in spite of himself, 'Omsk . . .'

'Is nothing fonny!'

'No, no of course not.' Great Uncle Bulgaria pulled himself together and glowered at Tobermory, who was now doubled up and making strange wheezing sounds. 'It's er – a – er – very fine name. Tobermory, behave yourself, do! Only you see Omsk, tck, tck, tck, Omsk, we'd thought that after all the messages you sent us that OW must stand for Other Womble. While all the time . . .'

'It was Omsk,' said Omsk coldly. 'Is not fonny.'

'No indeed. Er – why – Omsk – didn't you come out into the open before? We always knew you were around.'

'I was not sure that you were friendly Wumbles.'

'All Wombles are friendly towards other Wombles,' said Great Uncle Bulgaria in a very shocked voice. Omsk ducked his head and shuffled his large back paws and Tobermory, who had now managed to straighten up, said in a slightly muffled voice:

'I think we'd all better have a nice hot mug of acorn broth. Won't be a moment . . .'

'A good idea. Oh sit down, do!' said Great Uncle Bulgaria to Omsk. 'And stop all this saluting and heel-clicking

business. This is my burrow and I've no time for it. Now then Omsk Womble, why have you been spying on us and following us about and *why* did you warn us about Tomsk going under the ice, if you didn't mean to be friendly in the first place, eh? Ho hum?'

Omsk lifted his shoulders up to his ears and shrugged in a very expressive way.

'I never heard such rubbish,' said Great Uncle Bulgaria, exactly as if Omsk had gone into some long explanation.

'You young Wombles are all the same. You get some idea into your brains and there it sticks. You've no common sense at all. You might as well be Human Beings. You've come under the wire from the Embassy in Millionaire's Row – as I believe it's vulgarly named – haven't you? Well it's high time you realized that we Wombles don't hold with fences and all the rest of it, because we're all Wombles together. Ah, there you are Tobermory. I could do with a nice hot drink of acorn broth and I daresay you could too. Well Omsk, to use a toast of a very old friend of mine, the McWomble the Terrible, I look towards you!'

'What is?' asked Omsk glancing at Tobermory for help, as a great many Wombles did sooner or later.

'It means good health,' said Tobermory, 'drink up.'

They all three of them raised and chinked their mugs together and matters were really going very well; so it only needed Bungo to muddle everything up and, being Bungo, he *would* happen to choose that particular moment to appear in the doorway.

He was wearing what appeared to be some sort of long, white nightdress, while round his neck was a row of plastic bubbles.

'Great Uncle Bulgaria,' said Bungo, 'I've decided something.'

'Tck, tck, tck,' said Tobermory.

'Is fonny?' asked Omsk.

'Go on,' said Great Uncle Bulgaria with a deep sigh.

Bungo rattled the plastic bubbles.

'I'm giving up work,' he announced, 'I'm going to become the very first ever Hippy Womble.'

'Is fonny?' asked Omsk anxiously.

'Niet!' said Great Uncle Bulgaria

10

Dandelion omelette

'Chewy-crunchy-chocky,' murmured Orinoco, walking down the main corridor of the burrow with his head back as usual so that he could torture himself by reading the sweet papers on the ceiling. 'Whoops, look out Wellington.'

'Sorry,' said Wellington, 'but would you mind standing back. HE'S coming.'

The two Wombles flattened – well, did their best to flatten – their portly shapes against the side of the burrow as a strange figure came slowly into sight. It was Bungo, who was still wearing his long nightdress. He had added a row of small bells to his plastic bubble necklace, so that he tinkled as he moved; while perched on his nose was a pair of enormous square-shaped sunglasses with daisies threaded round the frames. He had brushed his fur down over his eyes, so that – what with one thing and another – it was impossible to tell if these were open or not. He certainly moved like a sleepwalker with his front paws held out before him.

Bungo stopped in front of the goggling Orinoco and turned the blank black stare of his sunglasses towards him. There was a long, uneasy silence, during which Orinoco could hear Madame Cholet humming to herself in the kitchen, the squeak-squeak of Great Uncle Bulgaria's rocking-chair, the chant of small voices in the Womble-garten as they recited:

'Wombles are *tidy* and Wombles are *neat*
They pick up the *rubbish* that lies in the street . . .'

While from Tobermory's Workshop there came a steady 'whir-whir-click-click-click'.

'Hallo ... whoo-*hoo*!' said Orinoco, unnerved by the weird behaviour of his old friend.

Bungo said nothing.

'What's he doing?' Orinoco whispered out of the corner of his mouth.

'Meditating,' said Wellington. '*Fonny* isn't it?' and he giggled.

'Not to me it isn't, I'm off ...'

And Orinoco, his back pressed to the side of the tunnel, slid off down the corridor and took refuge in his favourite place.

'Well, my little fat one,' said Madame Cholet. 'How are matters with you, eh?'

'Tricky.'

Orinoco produced a piece of folded paper out of the pocket of his workman-like apron and spread it across the scrubbed kitchen table. It was a blue print of the enormous stove and how it worked – or should work – and it was a silent testimony to Orinoco's determination. He was not a mechanically minded Womble, so it had taken him hours of concentration (and a helping paw from Tobermory) to produce this work of art. He thought of this now and he heaved a truly deep sigh as he said to no one in particular:

'It's very difficult to think properly on an empty stomach ...'

'Ho hum,' said Madame Cholet, 'well it so happens that I have just baked some batches of banana-skin biscuits. I suppose that out of thirty-six dozen one or two would not be missed, eh?'

'Shouldn't think so. Thanks ever so much, Madame Cholet ...'

There was a faint tinkling sound out in the passage and

Orinoco paused, a biscuit half-way to his open mouth. The tinkling passed on, grew fainter and disappeared.

'Tck, tck, tck,' said Madame Cholet, reaching up for one of her saucepans which was suspended from the spring mattress on the ceiling, 'le pauvre Bungo and le pauvre Wellington too, having to follow him about all day like a little sheepdog in order to stop him doing anything foolish. Another biscuit?'

'*Rather*. How long do you think it will last? Bungo being a Hippy Womble I mean?'

'Who can say?' Madame Cholet's shoulders rose about her ears in a truly French shrug. 'Bungo always throws himself with his whole heart into whatever he is about. He has eighty-four stars on the chart, so I hear. So obviously he has overworked himself . . .'

'Like me,' agreed Orinoco somewhat indistinctly through his fourth biscuit. Madame Cholet removed the tin and replaced the lid firmly, while Orinoco watched her regretfully.

'Like you,' said Madame Cholet, 'like Wellington and like Tomsk. It is a good thing that we now have this Omsk helping us. He eats even more than you – which I should not have believed possible – but he is a grrrrrreat worker. With

Bungo and Wellington off tidying up duty, the Park would be in a poor state were it not for this Omsk.'

Orinoco looked hopefully at the acorn juice which Madame Cholet was busy stirring.

'And please to continue with getting that new stove to work properly. It is most difficult for me to cook all the meals when Tobermory insists on these power cuts of his. Smell-Pollu indeed,' and Madame Cholet sniffed, 'since when has my food produced anything but truly delicious smells?'

'Never, *ever*,' Orinoco said fervently. 'Everything you cook is smashing. Particularly that acorn juice you're making now . . .'

'Get on with you,' said Madame Cholet giving him a friendly cuff round the ears, 'all right, a cup you may have . . .' And she reached up with a crackle of her starched apron and took a mug, with 'A Present From Blackpool' painted on it, off the dresser, saying over her shoulder, 'in the last few weeks, since you got the new cooker into the burrow, you have drunk enough of my acorn juice to sink a Serpentine boat. I don't believe that all those acorn grounds can be good for your inside, you know. Tobermory has promised that he will make a little machine for filtering them out, but at the moment he is too busy with this project of his.'

'What project?' asked Orinoco vaguely as he stared from his blue-print to the enormous stove and then back again.

'Who can say? When one inquires as to its nature Tobermory replies, "tick-tock, tick-tock. Heh, heh, heh." Here you are . . .'

'Thanks ever so. P'raps he's making a super clock, although I don't know what that'd have to do with fighting Pollu. Mmmm, it *does* smell nice.'

Orinoco picked up the steaming mug and went over to his stove. He had taken it to pieces and he had cleaned those

pieces to within an inch of their lives; and had straightened
out the bent bits and scrubbed away the rusty patches and
painted them; and had even, under the watchful eye of Tobermory, used the tools in the Workshop to make some new
parts. As he had never done anything of this kind before,
Orinoco was enormously proud of the gleaming, good-as-
new-if-not-better results of his labour.

There was, however, one slight snag.

This stove might be bigger and might prove to be more
efficient than the old one, but it still had the same drawback.
The smells, delicious though they were, of Madame Cholet's
cooking would still have to wind their way up through
the vent pipes in the ceiling and so ultimately into the
Park ...

Orinoco sipped, frowned, sipped again and glowered.
There was this large sort of chimney-thing built into the
back of the stove. And jutting out from the chimney-thing
was a kind of roof, like the roofs you saw on Human Beings'
houses, only smaller of course.

Still clutching his now half-empty mug Orinoco leant his
back against the stove and peered up into the roof. If only he
could capture the cooking smells *in* that roof and somehow
make them all vanish.

'Hm, hm, hm,' muttered Orinoco and went and got a
wooden stool that had 'ox's Orange Pippi' stamped across its
seat. He took it over to the stove and climbed upon to it
and, with this added height, he was able to get the whole top
half of himself inside the roof. It was rather dark, but Orinoco's little eyes soon adjusted to that and he ran one paw
round it, stuck his pink tongue out of the side of his mouth
and thought just about as hard as he had ever done in his
whole life.

'If there was something here ... something here ... something here ...' his own voice echoed round and round his
head and nearly made him lose his balance, 'to get hold of

the smells . . . smells . . . smells . . . Don't *do* that! . . . that . . . that . . .'

'Are you all right up there?' inquired Madame Cholet.

'Yes thanks . . . anks . . . anks . . . anks . . .' rumbled Orinoco and swigged down the rest of his drink, his mouth puckering as he swallowed some acorn grains. Madame Cholet was quite right! Grains couldn't possibly be good for a Womble's stomach. They were all gritty and bitty and they made your eyes water and they took away the nice taste and scent from the last drops of the juice . . .

'Yow!' said Orinoco and stepped forwards into space in his excitement as an idea burst into his mind. Naturally he came off the stool and found himself sitting on the floor, his mug held straight out in front of him, while Madame Cholet, with a wooden spoon in one paw and a saucepan in the other, said anxiously:

'You are all right? Speak to me Orinoco! Say something!'

'Acorn grains,' mumbled Orinoco. 'ACORN GRAINS!'

'You have choked on them?'

'Not half,' said Orinoco scrambling to his back paws, 'I'll say! Acorn GRAINS. Madame Cholet have you got any of them going spare?'

'The-you-what?' said Madame Cholet. 'Why yes. I have two old petrol drums full of them. Tobermory is going to take them away in a day or two. He says they make good compost. But why?'

'Good, good, good,' shouted Orinoco. 'Keep them. Guard them. They may be very, very, VERY important. All I need now is a tray with holes in it . . .'

'With holes in it . . .' repeated Madame Cholet, echoing Orinoco's words rather in the manner of the stove roof.

'Sort of holes. Only not big ones, because the grains'd come through. Won't be a tick.'

And Orinoco, with a burst of speed surprising in one of his

tubby build, whizzed out of the kitchen, leaving Madame Cholet staring after him. She shook her head a few times and then returned to her cooking with one eye on the clock, as she knew that a Tobermory power cut was coming shortly. The thought of this put everything else out of her head, for like all very good cooks, the importance of producing a meal dead on time was what really counted with her. So she didn't even turn round when Orinoco reappeared in the kitchen, dragging behind him a shining section of metal with a wire mesh grill in it, which had once upon a time been the open air side of a Human Being's outside larder.

'What are you doing, eh?' asked Madame Cholet, tasting and stirring everything that was bubbling and simmering on her old stove and inside its oven. 'A touch more moss salt perhaps and a soupçon of holly garlic. Well?'

'Working,' said Orinoco tersely. He had practically snatched a steel saw, a hammer, some small blocks of wood and a pot of glue out of Tobermory's paws and in a very few seconds that elderly Womble appeared in the doorway.

'Tck, tck, tck,' he said. 'Hold the saw straight, do, and that glue needs a good stir because its gone very thick at the bottom ...'

'Not in *my* kitchen!' said Madame Cholet turning round and brandishing a ladle at them. 'I am about to dish up and I will not have the pair of you hammering and sawing and making all kinds of dirt in here. Out, *out*, OUT!'

'She means it,' said Tobermory in a small voice. 'Better do what she says, young Womble.'

'But . . .'

'There are times,' said Tobermory sweeping the tools into his apron pocket and catching hold of Orinoco by the scruff of his neck, 'when it's better to give in. Sorry Madame Cholet, I'm sure . . .'

'And your dinners, eh?' Madame Cholet shouted after the retreating Wombles.

'Can you keep 'em warm?' suggested Tobermory and ducked just in time as a wooden spoon sailed over his grey head.

'It is fir-cone soufflé to start with. It will be ruined if it's not eaten at once!'

But for once Orinoco was deaf to this dreadful warning, which only went to show all over again just how hard he was concentrating. In fact the soufflé, their portions of it anyway, had sunk into a kind of grey pancake by the time Orinoco and Tobermory returned to the kitchen. While Madame Cholet, a most dignified expression on her face, had long since gone off to the Womblegarten to give them a domestic science lesson. Miss Adelaide sensed that something had upset her old friend's feelings, but she only sat quietly at the back of the classroom, her silky paws busy with another scarlet woolly pompom, for she knew very well that before the day was over, Madame Cholet would unburden all her grievances.

'Up a bit, round a bit, down a bit,' grunted Tobermory, who was now standing on the 'ox's Orange Pippi' stool, while Orinoco was actually balanced on the top of the stove.

With much groaning and grunting and heaving they got the reshaped wire mesh grill into place, so that it rested on the wood blocks they had glued inside the top of the stove roof. Their job was made rather more difficult because the grill was now covered in a thick mush of acorn grains.

'Hold on, hang on, steady . . .' grunted Orinoco, 'and down she comes . . . comes . . . comes . . . comes.'

'No need to repeat yourself, young Womble.'

'It wasn't me, it was the roof thing. Wait. Hallo . . .'

'Hallo,' echoed the roof, 'aallosh, aalloosh, ashoooo, shhhhh . . .'

'Well it certainly works from a sound point of view,' said Tobermory clambering down to floor level. 'So it only remains to be seen if it works as well from a *smell* point of view. I tell you what, young Womble. I'll switch on the

current and then I'll go above ground to where this particular chimney comes out into the Park and I'll sniff . . .'

'Sniff what?' asked Orinoco, a trace of suspicion in his voice as he slithered off the stove and dusted down his front paws.

'I'm glad you asked me that question,' said Tobermory from the doorway of the kitchen. 'Something nice and tasty. Something with a *particularly* delicious smell to it. I'd suggest that the best thing you can do is to consult Madame Cholet . . .'

'B . . . b . . . b . . . but,' stammered Orinoco.

'Courage, young Womble,' said Tobermory, a twinkle in his little black eyes, 'and if you want to win that Gold Medal, courage is what you are going to need. Tck, tck, tck . . .'

Orinoco looked round the empty kitchen . . . and then he looked at what had once been two portions of fir-cone soufflé . . . and then he looked at the enormous stove . . . and then he took his courage in both paws and went to look for Madame Cholet.

Madame Cholet was calm and quiet and dignified. She studied her scrubbed front paws, smoothed down her crackling apron and breathed deeply. Orinoco's fur stood up on end and his back paws made two quite distinct grooves in the floor of the Womblegarten, but somehow he managed to blurt out his request.

'Very well,' said Madame Cholet at last. 'You, and a certain other Womble – who should know better – have allowed two of my finest creations to become absolute ruins. Hard, leathery and uneatable. And when I took so much time over them! Soufflés, you understand, should be eaten *at once*. Eh?'

'Yes, I *do know*,' said Orinoco, with such a lot of feeling in his voice that Madame Cholet unbent a little. 'Pardonnez moi, Miss Adelaide,' she said and swept out of the Womblegarten and down the corridor, quite ignoring Bungo who was doing his sleepwalking act with Wellington trotting along behind him. Wellington looked at Orinoco who shrugged and then the two groups were past each other, although a faint tinkling sound followed Orinoco and Madame Cholet into the kitchen.

'Ah HA,' said Madame Cholet. 'And now what would you?'

'I would, I would, I mean would *you* please be kind enough to just mix up something extra nice and smelly. Just about the nicest, smelliest, thing you can think of actually, on the new stove. It *is* connected up.'

Madame Cholet paused. She had been extremely hurt by the way in which Orinoco and Tobermory had treated her beautiful soufflés, but on the other paw she could never resist a challenge.

'Bien,' said Madame Cholet and reached for her most precious pan, 'I will now make for you an omelette. An omelette fines herbes avec dandelion AND,' she took a deep breath as she reached for what had once been an ice-cream tub but was now relabelled. 'AND curried sycamore leaves. Yes?'

'Oooooh,' gasped Orinoco. 'RATHER. I'm starving . . .'

Within a matter of seconds Madame Cholet was at work, her paws moving at the speed of light as whisks spun, bowls rattled, saucepans hissed and her omelette pan glowed.

'Split – splat – splot . . .'

'Oooooooohh,' groaned Orinoco and even Bungo, who happened to be sleepwalking down the main burrow, paused and sniffed while Wellington, trundling along behind him, licked his lips. Omsk and Tomsk, returning to the burrow with two enormous plastic bags trailing behind them, stopped and looked at each other and the click-click of Great Uncle Bulgaria's rocking-chair came to a halt. Only Miss Adelaide went quietly on with the Womble fairy story she was reading to her pupils:

'So there was this terrible giant, called Pollu, who said, "I will swallow up the whole world . . ." '

'SPLAT!

'Mmmmmmm,' sighed Orinoco.

Madame Cholet turned her best pan this way and that and

slid two plates under the grill of the new stove. While up above ground Tobermory lay flat on his stomach, with his nose no more than two inches away from the place where the air vent from the new stove appeared from out of the ground in the middle of a bush.

'Sniff, sniff, sniff,' muttered Tobermory. 'No nothing. Poor old Orinoco. I suppose Madame Cholet *was* in a bit of a temper – I'll never understand cooks, not if I live to be *three* hundred – and so she wouldn't agree to our little experiment! Shame. Never mind . . .'

Tobermory got somewhat stiffly to his back paws and walked to the burrow entrance, nodding at Tomsk and Omsk who for some extraordinary reason were licking their lips, and went on his way.

'Here, Tobermory, old friend,' called out Great Uncle Bulgaria.

'Not now, if you don't mind,' said Tobermory and retired into his Workshop and began tinkering. He hadn't been doing it for more than ten seconds before Orinoco came bouncing into the room with his little black eyes shining like stars on a frosty night.

'Come on,' said Orinoco. 'Come *on*, Tobermory. Your dinner's getting cold for the second time. She's made something with a really STRONG smell!'

'You don't mean . . .?' Tobermory said slowly.

'I do,' said Orinoco, fairly bubbling over with excitement. 'Madame Cholet's cooked you – and me – two omelettes fines herbes avec dandelions and . . . *and* curried sycamore leaves. Didn't you smell it at all?'

'Not a whiff, said Tobermory. 'Not one *single* whiff. Are you sure you've got it right, young Womble?'

'RATHER,' said Orinoco, 'and do please hurry, Tobermory, or Madame Cholet may start throwing things again. You know what a state she gets into if we let meals get cold. Not that I often do, actually . . .'

'Tck, tck, tck,' said Tobermory. 'So it works. Congratulations, young Womble.'

Orinoco paused and in spite of the truly dreadful rumbling, empty feeling in his stomach he found himself saying:

'Well, yes. But I couldn't have done it, if you hadn't helped me ever such a lot.'

'Get on,' grunted Tobermory, 'there's no point in letting two sets of dinners get ruined. Goodness knows what Madame Cholet would say if we did. So shift yourself, young Womble, for goodness sake . . .'

11

Emergency! – Red Alert!

'So it looks as if Orinoco is going to win the Gold Medal,' said Great Uncle Bulgaria, who had been studying the star chart through first one pair of spectacles and then the other pair and finally through both of them. 'Although, old friend, I feel you had more than a paw in helping him to win all those extra marks.'

'Nonsense,' Tobermory replied, 'Orinoco had all the ideas. All he needed was a shove in the right direction. And anyway, what about Wellington's great discovery. Hm?'

'Ah, well, yes,' said Great Uncle Bulgaria. 'It was the same sort of situation really . . .'

'Tck, tck, tck,' said Tobermory, gazing in a very innocent way at the ceiling.

'Yes, yes, yes,' Great Uncle Bulgaria said hurriedly. 'Well, that's enough of *that*! How are Omsk and Tomsk getting along and what's the latest report on our Hippy Womble?'

Bungo's still meditating,' Tobermory said in a toneless voice, 'but that dratted Pop Festival ends today so we shall see *what* we shall see . . .'

'Meaning?'

'Meaning a quite extraordinary amount of rubbish down by the Serpentine. A mountain of it, I shouldn't be surprised. Tons and tons of litter probably. I *know* what these young Human Beings are like! Young Bungo's going through a silly sort of bit at the moment, but when he sees all that waste his Womble instincts will come to the surface. No, it's not him

I'm worried about,' and Tobermory scratched behind his grey ear with his screwdriver.

'Who then?'

'Wellington, Tomsk and Miss . . . no I'm not going to say any more. Enough's enough,' and Tobermory went stumping off to his Workshop, leaving Great Uncle Bulgaria looking after him.

'Ho *hum*,' said Great Uncle Bulgaria and shook out his today's edition of *The Times* and began to read the personal column.

A great many events now occurred almost on top of each other, but undoubtedly the first was the trouble with Tomsk. Right from their very first meeting he and Omsk had got on splendidly. Tomsk was not a curious or inquisitive Womble, and so he accepted the somewhat surprising addition of Omsk to the Hyde Park burrow without question. All he said was:

'Do you like swimming?'

'Da.'

'I suppose that's "yes" or something like it. O.K. Come and see the Serpentine. We've got awful Pollu problems there, you know, and the birds and the fish don't like it. Come to think of it, we've got some of your Russian geese knocking about, so it's your problem too . . .'

'How do you know they are Ross-ian?' asked Omsk in his deliberate way.

'By the snow on their feet,' said Tomsk and nearly fell over because he was laughing so much. 'Snow on their . . . oh never mind. Come on, I'll show you . . .'

About half an hour later, while the two of them were scooping up rubbish by the armful out of the Round Pond, Omsk suddenly started to make a noise like, 'Ho-ho-ho.'

'Have you swallowed something?' asked Tomsk.

'No,' said Omsk with a great roar of laughter. 'Snow on their feet! Is fonny. Ho, ho, ho . . .'

'Oh dear, oh me,' muttered Tomsk and returned to his work. It really was backbreaking work, too, because, although he and Omsk laboured from before dawn until well into the rush hour (with all its smelly petrol fumes) and again from dusk until nearly midnight, the birds and quite a number of the fish in the waters of Hyde Park and Kensington Gardens were still choking and gasping and poisoning themselves, not only with all the Pollu that was regularly being dumped in their feeding grounds, but also with the extra rubbish from the Pop Festival.

'Is no good,' said Omsk, plonking himself down on the Serpentine Road by the light of the silvery moon. 'Hush off, you . . .'

'It's only Hoo-Hoo,' said Tomsk. 'He's O.K. But you're right. All we can do is tidy up all the rubbish that floats about on the surface. Da?'

(Tomsk was getting quite good at Russian.)

'Da,' agreed Omsk. 'In Ross-ia we have no such problem.'

'I bet you jolly well do.'

'Well, only small problem.'

'Get on.'

'Which, yes, grows larger. But we Ross-ian Wumbles have great system. We use sheeps.'

'Ba-ba sheeps?'

'Niet, niet, niet. Sheeps with sail-ers.'

'Oh that sort of sheep – I mean ship. With *sails*. I see – I think.'

'And ne-ets.'

'Nets,' said Tomsk. 'Jolly good idea too. Sailing ships with nets. Yes, I suppose that would work. *If* one had a ship and a net. Or if one could *make* a ship and a net. I say Omsk, old Wumble-Womble, I think we might be on to something. We'd better talk to Tobermory. Da?'

'Build a *ship*!' said Tobermory, coming out of his

Workshop and scratching his ear with what looked like a large clockwork key instead of his usual screwdriver. 'I don't know much about ships. Boats, yes, but . . .'

'A boat'd probably be just as good,' said Tomsk. 'Eh Omsk, old Wumble?'

'Ho hum,' agreed Omsk, bowing and smiling and clicking his heels. 'Bo-at. Da!'

'Get along to the library then,' said Tobermory, who, in his own mind was treating the whole idea as a joke. 'Bungo's in there "meditating" – lot of nonsense – but Wellington's with him and he'll know what books to sort out for you, I shouldn't wonder. . .'

Wellington was only too delighted to help, as he had now been on light duties (following Bungo around) for several days and was getting rather bored. His overworked brain having had a good rest – which was exactly what Great Uncle Bulgaria had planned – he was now only too anxious to start thinking again, so he scurried about the shelves and in hardly any time at all presented Omsk and Tomsk with an armful of books ranging from *How to make a Canoe* to *Build your own Cabin cruiser.*

'Is good,' growled Omsk. 'Now we are comrades, yes?' and he leant across the table holding out a large paw. 'Am sorry if I frighten you in your laboratory-tory. But was inter-es-eted in your experiments. Da?'

'That's O.K.,' said Wellington, shaking away for all he was worth, 'but you know I'd have asked you in if I'd known who you were. Sorry.'

'Is my fault,' said Omsk rather sadly, 'I have become rather a sur-spicious Wumble. Tck, tck, tck.'

'Tck, tck, tck,' agreed Wellington. 'Well, it's all over and done with now. Come along, Bungo. Meditating time's over . . . and what's more,' and his bright little eyes went to the clock, 'that Pop Festival of yours has just finished, so we'd better go and have a look at the site . . .'

It was a sight to make even the bravest Womble heart quail, a sight to turn blood as cold as an iced-lolly, a sight to make fur prickle, noses twitch and eyes screw themselves tight shut in the hope that the nightmare would go away.

The stretch of land where the Festival had taken place looked as if all the green Royal Parks rubbish collecting vans had decided to unload themselves there. Overnight, or so it seemed, a new rubbish dump had come into being.

'Oh my,' whispered Wellington, 'oh my, *oh my*, OH MY!'

There were bottles and soft drink tins by the thousand. There were newspapers and magazines and books and posters and sweet wrappers and paper tissues and just crumpled sheets of paper. There were battered plastic containers of every shape, colour and size. There were empty boxes and packets and plastic mugs and milk bottles and knives, forks, spoons and plates. There were torn groundsheets and coats and shoes and sandals and raffia bags and shopping baskets and hats, caps and berets. There were iced-lolly sticks, ice-cream cartons and sunglasses and ordinary glasses and long playing records, record sleeves and bits out of transistor radios. There were handbags and wallets and flags and strings of beads and plastic flowers. There were cushions and punctured air-beds and torn nylon quilts and thermos flasks and cardboard cartons. There were pens and pencils and biros and felt tips. There were corks and bottle-tops and tin-openers and small paraffin picnic stoves and paraffin tins. There were apple cores and pear cores and banana skins and orange skins and eggshells and melon rinds and plum stones and bits of bread, cakes and sandwiches. There were broken watches, clocks and torches. There were – but it's too depressing to go on.

And, worst of all, flies, blue-bottles and wasps were humming round this great mountain of rubbish, and every now and again, as the horrified Wellington stared and stared,

there would be a small avalanche as a grey sewer rat went scavenging for some delicious rotting morsel. Like the insects they had been drawn by the faint but increasing smell of decay, which was starting to rise like a mist over this man-made battlefield of Pollu.

'I can't believe it,' whispered Wellington and rubbed his eyes with his paws.

'Back to the burrow,' said a brisk voice at his side. 'No time to lose!'

Wellington jumped and looked and then looked again. Bungo had removed his nightgown and his beads, bells and sunglasses and was brushing the fur out of his eyes. All traces of the Hippy Womble had completely vanished and Bungo was very much his old self again.

'Come on,' he said. 'Jump to it, young Wellington. If we don't act quickly we'll have half the sewer rats in London here in a few hours . . .'

'We can't clear up all that,' Wellington almost wailed.

But Bungo was already running for dear life, not towards the rubbish, but back towards the burrow. He rushed past Tomsk and Omsk, who with a book apiece in their paws were gravely considering Tomsk's pile of white plastic bits. He muttered 'morning, morning, morning . . .' to Madame

Cholet, Miss Adelaide and Tobermory who had all come out of their respective workrooms to see what all the running was about, and he knocked on Great Uncle Bulgaria's door and was inside that room, before the old Womble had even said 'come in'.

'And what . . . .' began Great Uncle Bulgaria sternly, looking up from his desk where he was pasting little bits of paper on to a sheet of cardboard. 'All right, young Bungo, I can see something startling has occurred, but try and pull yourself together and tell me calmly what it is all about. I am relieved to see that you have divested yourself of those ridiculous clothes, and I can only presume that this shows you are no longer a Hippy Womble . . .'

'Hippy!' said Bungo, who by this time had got some of his breath back. 'Ha! You should just see the mess they've made. They've left tons and *tons* and TONS of litter down by the Serpentine – the most litter I've ever seen in my whole life – and the rats and the blue-bottles are down there already. We'll never clear it all up, never . . .'

'I see. Well we must do what we can in order to stop contamination. Sound the big warning bell and call everybody – even the Womblegarten – into the recreation room. Everyone is to drop whatever they are doing and to go there immediately. Now jump to it.'

Bungo jumped. So did everybody else, because they all knew that the Womble Alarm bell was only rung in emergencies.

'Now listen to me,' said Great Uncle Bulgaria to the rows and rows of furry faces before him. 'This is no time for me to make a speech (Tobermory breathed a faint sigh of relief) . . . Much as I should like to. A great many tons of very mixed litter have been left behind by the Serpentine. By the time the sun comes up we shall have some really bad smell-Pollu on our paws, and with it will come the dangers of germs, bugs and diseases. So I'm declaring this a crisis and

we shall *all* be on full Red Alert. Tobermory, you will organize parties of tidying up Wombles and issue them with the largest tidy-bags we have ...'

'We could use prams and wheelbarrows as well ...'

'Good idea. Miss Adelaide, I put you in charge of the Womblegarten, who will sort the rubbish as it arrives.'

'Certainly, Great Uncle Bulgaria,' said Miss Adelaide calmly. But her little black eyes were shining with pride and excitement. At last her young Wombles were going to be truly involved in the fight against Pollu!

'And as for me,' said Madame Cholet with a fat chuckle, '*I* know! I am to turn my kitchen into a canteen. And possibly a first-aid centre – should anyone get cut, bitten or scratched. Yes?'

'Yes. Thank you. Right,' and Great Uncle Bulgaria clapped his paws. 'Action stations and good luck!'

The next few hours were something of a blur to the Wombles. They were all used to working hard, but now it seemed as though there were hardly time to breathe. The first working party was hard at it within five minutes – a long line of trotting Wombles, some of them clasping bags and shovels, others pushing wheelbarrows and prams. The rats swarmed out of the dump in their dozens and went skittering off, red-eyed and furious. The blue-bottles, wasps and fleas rose in their hundreds and thousands and then zoomed down again, buzzing and biting.

'Get off,' muttered Tomsk, shaking his head violently as he staggered up the slope with a load of tins which was as big as himself. 'Can't *you* do something about it, you great gormless bird ... get off wasp!'

Hoo-Hoo looked hurt, halted and then took to his wings and went flying back to the dump and began to swoop up and down it. Within a few seconds he was joined by some ducks and then some sparrows and then a great flock of starlings. They dived on the buzzing insects and at the same time the fish, led by the old carp, started to rise to the surface of the water, their jaws opening and closing, so that insects who escaped from the birds were soon vanishing into those fishy jaws.

But the Wombles hardly noticed; they were too busy to do anything but concentrate on their own particular patch, and when one of them paused for a quick snack or a cooling drink they were too bemused to speak. Omsk was the only one who seemed to have any breath left for talking and all he muttered was:

'Is not fonny. Niet ...'

At the very furthest end of the burrow a group from the Womblegarten, under the direction of Miss Adelaide, were frantically digging a deep pit. As the Wombles are great burrowing creatures this pit went down at an enormously fast rate. A trotting line of little Wombles were taking the dug up earth out of the burrow in old fire buckets and spreading it neatly on the surrounding flower-beds. Tobermory, when Miss Adelaide managed to catch him for an instant, supplied a whole box of large, wooden clothes-pegs and a hammer, and two small Wombles drove these into the side of the pit to form a series of paw-holds which could be used as steps.

'And what is that pit for?' inquired Great Uncle Bulgaria, who in some mysterious way seemed to be everywhere at once encouraging, helping and directing.

'Unusable plastic objects,' said Miss Adelaide crisply, 'those that are beyond repair. We intend to dissolve them with a judicious amount of Wellington's Dis A stroke 3 and Dis Y stroke 2.'

'Excellent, excellent,' said Great Uncle Bulgaria. 'Well done, Miss Adelaide and all you young Wombles . . .'

The old Womble stumped off and had a look in at the kitchen. The enormous stove was going at full blast and the long scrubbed table held plate after plate of biscuits (banana skin), buns (orange peel with a pinch of sweet moss and with lemon peel topping), grassbread sandwiches (filled with creamy toadstool spread) and, a particular Womble delicacy, chilled eggshell consommé.

'Don't bother me now,' said Madame Cholet who was applying a fermented dockleaf lotion to Wellington, who had been stung by a wasp on the back of his paw. 'Help yourself to what you want from the table. The sycamore squash is in

the refrigerator. Oh, so it is *you*, Great Uncle Bulgaria. How does it march?'

'Very well indeed, Madame Cholet. I don't know how we'd have managed without you. A Womble, after all, *marches* on his stomach. A bientôt.'

'Alors,' agreed Madame Cholet.

Tobermory, with a screwdriver behind one grey ear and a pencil behind the other, was marking off a long list:

'Bottles, 234, in good condition. Yes. Bottles, 139, chipped, yes. Bottles, 63, unusable, yes. Allocate to crushing machine.'

'Crushing machine?' inquired Great Uncle Bulgaria.

'Garden roller Bungo brought in some time ago. Cumbersome, but effective. Later on I intend to mechanize it. Soft drinks tins, 2,310 – good grief!'

It *is* an amazingly high figure,' agreed Great Uncle Bulgaria. 'How are things going, old friend?'

'Busy. But I think we're winning. I haven't had time to work out any real figures, but on a rough reckoning I'd say there was around forty tons, FORTY TONS, of rubbish dumped down by the Serpentine. And that was just one week's worth of dumping. If you ask me, Bulgaria, the human race has gone mad. They'll choke themselves to death in the end. I'll never understand them. Not if I live to be *three* hundred!'

'Yes. I agree with you. They're beginning to see the problem – which *they* have created – but whether they'll learn how to deal with it quickly enough remains to be seen.'

'Um,' said Tobermory. 'Paper for repulping, 137 loads, yes. Plastic containers, assorted sizes, good condition, 219, yes . . . sorry you were saying?'

But Great Uncle Bulgaria had already departed and was now outside the burrow and surveying the scene before him. To his right was a long line of Wombles staggering up the slope with crammed tidy-bags, and loaded wheelbarrows and prams. To his left was another line of Wombles on their way down to the rubbish mountain, with empty containers of all kinds clutched in their weary paws. Bungo toiled past with a great plastic bag over his shoulder, his black eyes fixed firmly on the ground as he muttered:

'A hundred and two steps, a hundred and three steps, a hundred and . . .'

Orinoco passed him on the downward trail, an empty go-kart bumping ahead of him, while a few yards to his rear came Wellington, the cold compress still on his paw as he trundled along a large pram.

Omsk and Tomsk, side by side, were returning to the

burrow, dragging behind them a groundsheet which bulged with paraffin stoves, drums and bits of machinery.

'Dum, dum, dum, dum, dum-dum . . .' they were humming to the tune of the *Volga Boatmen*. 'Dum dum dum dum dum DUM dum dum dum . . .'

While as for the mountain of rubbish, it had been reduced to a shadow of its former self, and was now just a litter of bits and pieces in which the sparrows, starlings and some of the ducks were pecking busily. The heron was standing on one leg, looking at nothing in particular, and Hoo-Hoo was sailing up and down the Serpentine in a majestic fashion with only the old carp for company. There was no sign at all of a rat or even a blue-bottle, and the fresh clean air of the early morning had dispersed the evil smell of rotting rubbish.

'Not bad, not bad at all,' said Great Uncle Bulgaria.

He watched the golden light of the sun come streaking across the Park and then turned to look at the traffic which was already growing thicker and thicker. The first of the green-coloured rubbish lorries appeared in the gateway of the Royal Parks Office block and a mounted policeman started trotting along Rotten Row.

'Well, it's over to you now,' muttered Great Uncle Bulgaria, 'you can clear up the remains, but how you Human Beings would manage without *us* I tremble to think! Hallo, there comes the Superintendent's car. He seems a nice sort of person, even if he is human! Well, that's that then. I think I'll declare a twenty-four hour rest period. My Wombles have done remarkably well. Ho hum . . .'

Great Uncle Bulgaria returned home and, with a surprising agility in one of his age, sounded the 'Return to Burrow' on the Womble Alarm bell.

'And about time, too,' sighed Bungo.

'Get on,' said Wellington and in spite of being so tired that he was rocking on his back paws, he managed to add.

'Anyway, I thought you were the Womble who was so keen on all this meditation and Beautiful Living lark?'

It was lucky for Bungo that Great Uncle Bulgaria was not around to hear his reply. Otherwise he might have been sent to Coventry for at least a week.

12   The Gold Medal winner

After the red alert a somewhat lethargic feeling descended on the burrow. There was still a great deal of sorting to be done of course and a lot of reclamation, so that Tobermory was, as usual, kept busy from dusk till dawn, in spite of Great Uncle Bulgaria's strenuous efforts to stop him.

'You're overdoing it, old friend,' he said, looking at Tobermory's red-rimmed eyes and somewhat straggly fur. 'There's plenty of time . . .'

'No there isn't,' said Tobermory obstinately. 'For a start I've got 4032 Poppi-cola tins in the stores at this moment. They've all got to be cleaned or flattened and . . .'

'Tck, tck, tck,' said Great Uncle Bulgaria and went to have a word with Madame Cholet. The outcome of their little talk was that Tobermory, after his good-day drink of hot holly-berry broth, felt quite amazingly sleepy. So sleeply indeed that he slept the clock round twice and, during that time, Omsk and Tomsk invaded his back Workshop and put their own secret project into action. Tobermory would have had a fit if he could have seen them, and he would certainly have tried to get a paw in the works. But he wasn't here, so Omsk and Tomsk were able to go their own way.

'Are you sure is O.K.?' mumbled Omsk.

'Yes, yes, yes. Wellington's worked out all the arithmetic bits and he's ever so clever, you know, and then we've got our plans and Bungo's crusher and the use of Orinoco's

enormous stove to heat up the white mud. It's certain to be all right . . .'

'If Great Little Uncle Bulgaria does not discover,' said Omsk.

During the last few weeks he had learnt a great deal. When he had first been welcomed into the burrow he'd had grave doubts about the Hyde Park Wombles. All of them, it had seemed to him, could shove their paws in anywhere they chose. Take for instance the case of Orinoco and his stove. Why should he have been allowed to try it out in that haphazard way? And then Bungo had been allowed to become a Hippy Womble without anybody trying to stop him. What was more he had been almost encouraged; for no Womble had tried to interfere with his meditating or had tried to make him work. Indeed Wellington had been taken off his own important scientific duties in order to follow Bungo around. It was all most disturbing and irregular. Particularly as it appeared to produce such excellent results!

'In Rossia,' rumbled Omsk, 'should a Wumble want to start a project such as this one, he would first of all have to draw up his plans and then submit them to his Workroom Leader. Workroom Leader would then call meeting of his staff. If plans were O.K. they would then be passed to Burrow Leader. Burrow Leader would then call meeting. After which . . .'

'Really?' said Tomsk, who hadn't been listening to a word of this. 'Now then we've got all the white polystyrene stuff, so start crushing . . .'

It was a good thing that Omsk and Tomsk were the two largest and strongest Wombles in the burrow, for the next few hours were very tough going. So, when Bungo's bright, inquisitive little face just happened to appear round the back Workshop door, and he just happened to inquire if there was anything he could do to help (and what was that stuff that looked like snow?), he found himself involved in the project too.

Naturally Orinoco came looking for Bungo and, before he could back out, Omsk had him firmly by the fur at the back of his neck, and had set him to stirring the powdery 'snow' into a large tin bath, which held some of Wellington's warm white sticky mud. And five minutes after that Wellington came bustling in with the excuse that he wanted to go through some of the figures he'd worked out for the project, and in no time flat he was laying delightfully soggy lumps of the 'snow' on the now mended groundsheets, and pounding at them with a large wooden spoon.

'It's like being back in the Womblegarten, isn't it?' said Bungo. 'Except there we were only allowed to make little things.'

'I wish *this* was a bit littler,' replied Orinoco, who was patting and smoothing with his paws at the strange object they were making. It was starting to resemble a bath with two sharp corners at one end and a wide, flat shelf at the other. 'I say, Wellington old chap, are you *sure* you've got the plan right?'

'Um, um, um,' said Wellington, his tongue sticking out of the side of his mouth. He wasn't at all sure, but it was too late to change anything as the sticky stuff was already beginning to set hard.

'I think it's jolly good,' said Tomsk, who with Omsk was pounding away at the flat end.

'Um, um, um,' said Wellington. He took a ruler out of his apron pocket and very carefully measured the 'bath' to find the dead centre of it; and then he put a particularly soggy mound of stuff in the middle, shaped it slightly and then reached over and picked up a tent pole which he rammed down into the mound and patted firmly into position.

'That's not very high, is it?' asked Tomsk doubtfully.

'Course not. If I made it the right height we'd never get it out of the burrow,' replied Wellington. 'But you see that metal bit at the top end of the pole? Well you fix another bit of pole into that. That's how tent poles work you know!'

'You really are clever,' said Bungo.

'Is scientific brain,' rumbled Omsk and dealt Wellington an affectionate pat which nearly sent that small Womble half-way across the Workshop.

'Now we've got to leave it for twenty-four hours,' said Tomsk, 'so that it can set quite hard. It does look a *bit* funny, but it's jolly good just the same. Thanks everybody . . .'

'Supposing Tobermory comes in and finds it?' asked Bungo.

'He won't,' said Tomsk. 'He hardly ever uses this back part of the Workshop . . .'

So it was just their hard luck that the following day Tobermory, now much refreshed after his long sleep, *did* go into the back of the Workshop to get something he needed for his own particular project. When he saw what was standing, so to speak, on the middle of the floor he thought for a moment that he must still be fast asleep and dreaming. He was still staring at it when Tomsk and Omsk came bustling in with excited expressions, which changed to worried ones when they saw their secret had been discovered.

'Hallo, Tobermory,' said Tomsk in a small voice, 'feeling better?'

'I was. Until I saw this – this *thing*. If it's not asking too much, *if* you don't think I'm being impertinent, *if* you don't mind my inquiring who gave you permission to use the back of my Workshop and *if* I may be so bold WHAT IS IT?'

'Is a sheep,' said Omsk.

'A sheep? Ah. I thought it might be some kind of two-headed swan.'

'Oh, Tobermory, *don't*,' said Tomsk, 'I'm awfully sorry I didn't ask permission, but we did clean up all the tools and things afterwards. And of course it's not a sheep or a swan. It's a,' he cleared his throat, 'it's a Wombleran. That's a sort of boat.'

'Is it?' said Tobermory, in the same sort of wondering voice he had used before. Then, as he had the kindest of hearts under his sometimes gruff exterior, he added, 'well, it's certainly a very remarkable object. Very remarkable indeed. Will it float? How do you steer it? And this I suppose is the mast, yes most ingenious. Ho hum.'

He was very tempted to tell them that, with a little adjustment *here* and a bit of reshaping *there*, they might have made a more stylish and perhaps even a safer craft. But as it was very unlikely that the Serpentine would ever produce gale force waves (and even should the Wombleran turn turtle, it wouldn't matter as all Wombles are excellent swimmers), Tobermory kept these thoughts to himself and only said:

'*Truly* remarkable, I'd no idea you'd taken up boating, Tomsk. Is it in honour of our outing?'

'No,' said Tomsk, his eyes starting to shine. 'It's my – our – project. I'm going to use one of those nylon quilts for a sail and that net curtain I found as a net. I'm going to trawl for rubbish! You know, Tobermory, I *did* tell you that the fish and the birds don't like all the Pollu in the water. Well, with my net I can tidy up lots more than I could just by paw, can't I?'

'Yes, indeed,' said Tobermory. 'Did you think of it all by yourself, Tomsk?'

Tomsk nodded violently. He knew he wasn't clever like Wellington or even like Bungo or Orinoco, so he really felt quite shivery that he'd had an idea all of his own.

'Course everybody else helped,' he said. 'I couldn't have done it without them. I mean Wellington did the drawings and Bungo . . .'

'Ho hum,' said Tobermory, 'I understand. But the main thing's it's your idea. Well done, Tomsk, young Womble. I must say I'm looking forward to the launching . . .'

'A WHAT?' said Great Uncle Bulgaria when Tobermory called in on him later. He had just finished sticking the last little bits of newspaper to the sheet of cardboard. He now wiped his paws on his handkerchief and looked over the top of his spectacles at Tobermory.

'Wombleran,' Tobermory said in a voice that was not quite steady, because he was trying not to laugh. 'Good gracious, Bulgaria old friend, surely you know what a Wombleran is! Tck, tck, tck . . .'

And he slipped out of the room before Great Uncle Bulgaria could think of an answer.

It was decided that the Wombleran should be launched as part of the outing festivities. A great feeling of excitement and anticipation was running through the burrow, as nobody yet knew who had won the Gold Medal, but the contest was now closed and the board had been taken down. Naturally everybody said that they were sure *they* hadn't won it.

'You're bound to get it, old chap,' Bungo said to Wellington, 'I mean you invented that stuff for melting plastic and making it vanish.'

'Oh no,' Wellington shook his head, 'it's sure to go to Orinoco for his enormous stove . . .'

'Who me? *Never*!' said Orinoco. 'I mean the stove was nothing really! It might be enormous, but it's almost a *little* idea compared to old Tomsk's Wombleran.'

'That's jolly nice of you,' said Tomsk, 'but I don't know yet if it'll even float properly. I think Miss Adelaide and the Womblegarten should get the Medal and kind of share it out – for digging that pit and doing all that sorting out.'

'Tck, tck, tck,' said Miss Adelaide. 'Naturally I'm most grateful for your kind thoughts. But it's my belief that young Bungo will be the winner. He, after all, had the most stars for collecting the most rubbish . . .'

'No,' said Bungo, trying hard to look modest and not succeeding at all, 'it'll be one of you. I'm sure it will.'

He was quite wrong. They all were . . .

The evening of the outing, the launching and the presentation was warm and full of silvery moonlight. As all the Wombles had had a good day's sleep they were bright-eyed and fairly bursting with excitement as they trooped out of the burrow, clutching in each paw a tidy-bag containing their picnic supper and a bottle of Madame Cholet's extra specially delicious fizzy mint-dandelionade.

There were 'ooohs' and 'aaaahs' all round when Omsk and Tomsk came down the bank to the Serpentine with the Wombleran, shrouded in a dust-sheet, held above their heads. Very gently they put it down on the bank and then Tomsk took a deep breath and said in a husky voice:

'Will you launch it please, Great Uncle Bulgaria?'

'Certainly. I should be most honoured. By the way has it a – er – a special name?'

'Yes,' said Tomsk, fairly bursting with excitement, 'and it's a surprise. Look . . .' And he pulled off the sheet and

everybody pressed forward and there were a whole lot more 'oooohs' and 'aaaahs' and everybody clapped.

All except Omsk, who just stood there with his mouth wide open.

'I name this ship,' said Great Uncle Bulgaria, tapping it with his own special bottle of extra-strong mint juice, 'I name this ship, the s.s. OMSK and good luck to all who sail in her!'

He gave it a little push and the Wombleran slid onto the water, bobbed about a bit and then sat there placidly, looking remarkably like a two-headed Hoo-Hoo.

'Is very kind,' said Omsk in a deep, deep rumble. 'Is . . .' And then he stopped, blew his nose and gave Tomsk a pat on the back which made even that large Womble rock on his back paws.

'Yes, yes, yes,' said Great Uncle Bulgaria. 'Now then, Wombles, I have a few words I wish to say to you. Where's my rostrum? Thank you.'

He stepped up onto the 'ox's Orange Pippi' stool and then placed his sheet of cardboard and the gold star chart on a music-stand, which Bungo, in a most important and bustling way, adjusted to the correct height.

'First of all,' said Great Uncle Bulgaria, 'I wish to say how proud, how *very* proud I am of all and everyone of you for the great fight you have put up against the Giant Pollu. You have fought the enemy in many ways. By collecting an amazing amount of rubbish . . .

Bungo stared fixedly at his back paws while Orinoco gave him a slight nudge.

'By making a truly remarkable discovery which gets rid of unusable plastic . . .'

It was Tomsk's turn to nudge Wellington, whose spectacles by this time were completely misted over.

'By thinking of and carrying through a new method of combating water-Pollu . . .'

Tomsk's knees buckled and Omsk had to hold him up.

'And by getting rid – and please excuse these words, Madame Cholet, as they are in no way a reflection of your excellent cooking . . .'

'Tiens,' said Madame Cholet and chuckled fatly.

'By getting rid of the trouble we had with the old stove – a project that was carried through by a Womble who has, perhaps, even more interest than the rest of us in his food . . .'

There was a lot of laughter and Orinoco was nudged by Bungo and several others.

'And I must further mention the remarkable work done by Miss Adelaide and her Womblegarten. Without them we could never had managed as well as we did during the Red Alert.'

All the working Wombles clapped and Miss Adelaide smoothed her silky grey paws and nodded to the members of the Womblegarten, who all scrambled to their back paws and ducked their small, soft furry heads.

'However,' said Great Uncle Bulgaria, who was really enjoying himself enormously. 'Before I proceed to the Prize Giving I should like to read out to you some messages which have been sent to me from all over the world by other Womble Communities. When I first announced Womble Conservation Year to you here in the Hyde Park burrow, I also inserted a small announcement in the personal column of *The Times*. It read: "Womble Conservation Year. Wombles of the World unite. Unite and fight pollution on land, in the sea and in the air! Signed Bulgaria Coburg Womble." Here are some of the responses I have received. "The Wombles of the United States are with you all the way. Warmest best wishes. Cousin Yellowstone." "Chinese Womble Republic have saying. There is no want where nothing is wasted. Greetings. Chairman Womble Wong." The next message is perhaps rather unusual. It comes from

Tibet and it says: "Salutations. What is pollution? Yeti-Womble." '

'What a smashing place to live,' whispered Orinoco. 'I know it's all jolly interesting, but I do *wish* Great Uncle Bulgaria would get on with announcing the winner!'

Orinoco hastily subsided as Great Uncle Bulgaria's sharp old eyes came to rest on him. The old Womble went on reading out the messages, well aware that the tension was now almost unbearable but, being an expert at public speaking, he kept his audience on their toes until, with a dramatic flourish, he put down his cardboard sheet and withdrew from inside his shawl a flat gold disc which glinted in the moonlight.

There was a sharp intake of breath on all sides and then absolute silence.

'After long and careful thought,' said Great Uncle Bulgaria, 'I have reached my decision. I have chosen a winner who has produced an idea which fights pollution on two levels. Noise and smell. Look . . .'

And he swept his white front paw in a half circle and pointed to the far end of the Serpentine Road. For a moment there was nothing to see and then out of the shadows came the large, sleek shape of the Wombles' own car, the Silver Womble. It came towards them as silently as a ghost although, as it came to a halt, those with the sharpest ears just managed to hear a faint 'tick-tock-tick-tock-tick-tock.'

'The first, the very first, full-sized clockwork car and driving it – the Womble who invented it and the winner of the Gold Medal – Tobermory!'

The idea of a car or a motor-bike, a lorry or a van which could be both quiet and not at all smelly was so extraordinary that none of the Wombles could take it in for some moments. How strange – and wonderful – it would be not to have that endless rumble of traffic and, even better, how marvellous it would be *not* to run the risk of picking up

'diesel paw' or coughing and spluttering because of fumes.

It took quite a bit of getting used to and then Wellington, who hated noise, began to clap and Orinoco, who hated smells (except particularly delicious *cooking* smells), started to clap too and then there was a perfect thunder of applause as Tobermory, at his gruffest, came forward to accept the medal. Nobody, not even Bungo, felt disappointed at not having won; for not only was Tobermory's invention quite astonishing, but he had also helped and given a willing paw to so many of them while they were working on their own projects.

'For he's a jolly good Womble,
For he's a jolly good Womble,
For he's a jolly good Womble and so say all of us ...'

'Tck, tck, tck,' said Tobermory and waved his front paw and then stumped off to go and sit beside Miss Adelaide.

'And because you've all worked so hard and so well,' said

Great Uncle Bulgaria, 'if you look in your tidy-bags you will find a little something to show my appreciation . . .'

And, sure enough, in the bottom of each bag was a large, round, flat toffeebark chocolate wrapped in silver paper.

'A silver medal!' said Bungo. 'I shall keep it for ever and ever.'

'I shan't,' said Orinoco, 'ooo, chewy, crunchy, chocky . . . Here steady on! Oi, let go of my arm, Bungo . . .'

'Come on,' said Bungo, 'Tobermory's lining everybody up for the first swimming race. It's Womble paddle and – between you and me – I've been doing a bit of practice. Picking up all that old rubbish has made my muscles ever so strong, look!' and Bungo flexed his front paw. 'Tomsk is smashing at the crawl, but Womble paddle just isn't his stroke. I bet I win!'

And, for once in his life, he was right!

THE LAST OF THE DRAGONS AND SOME OTHERS

E. Nesbit

'I know what it is,' said Effie. 'It is a dragon like St George killed.' And Effie was right, the winged creature that came crawling out of the boot really was a little dragon. In fact, there were 'winged lizards' appearing all over the country, though the newspapers of course never called them dragons for fear of looking silly.

As E. Nesbit cheerfully remarks, 'No one believes in dragons nowadays,' but by the time you have read a few of these stories you may be pretty well convinced – after all, if dragons *weren't* real, how could the author know such a lot about them and the different ways clever people have outwitted them?

A NECKLACE OF RAINDROPS

Joan Aiken

'Well!' said Aunt Lou. 'I thought of living in plenty of places, but I never thought of living up in the sky! What shall we find to eat up here?'

'That's easy,' Emma said, and it was easy too. The fact is the many impossible things seemed easy with an imagination and a storytelling power like Joan Aiken's. And never more so than in this collection of beautiful, scintillating, magical, poetical dreams and fancies which are very likely the necklace of raindrops in the title story.

MY FRIEND MR LEAKEY

J. B. S. Haldane

Mr Leakey was the only magician who could bring a sock to life, or bewitch a tie-pin and a diary so that he could never lose them. He wanted to run over to Java after lunch, and was going to use a touch of invisibility in the morning to cure a dog that was always biting people.

If you want to know more about Mr Leakey and his household jinn and the octopus who served his meals and the dragon (wearing asbestos boots) who grilled the fish, you must read this book to find out.

For readers of eight and over, especially boys.

THE MAGIC PUDDING

Norman Lindsay

This is a very funny book, about a very peculiar pudding. In spite of the word 'magic' in the title, there are no fairies or spells. Only a pudding.

Sometimes it was a rich odoriferous steak-and-kidney pudding, sometimes it was boiled jam roll or apple dumpling. All you had to do was whistle twice, turn the pudding round, and you could have whatever you wanted! Indeed the pudding was such a prize that there were 'professional puddin'-owners' and, alas, 'professional puddin' thieves'. One of the owners was Sam Sawnoff, whose feet were sitting down while his body was standing (he was a penguin), although Bill was just an ordinary small man with a large hat.

For ages eight to eighty, allowing for brief blind periods now and again in between.